THE ARROW PLODDED UP TO SEVEN AND STOPPED. THE ELEVATOR KEPT ON GOING.

It was the strangest sensation—as if the elevator was forcing its way up through something sticky in the shaft, like molasses or chewing gum. There was a thin humming noise all around Susan, and the light dimmed. She was startled, and a little frightened. But of course there were only seven floors, so the elevator would have to stop at the seventh. The arrow must be out of order. . . .

Then the elevator stopped. The door said "Sighhh . . ." and opened. Susan clutched her hands together and said, "Oh!"

"It is all very delightful and a lot of children and some grownups are going to believe it."
—Starred review, *School Library Journal*

"A light, enjoyable fantasy written with such adroitness that the author has, with success, put himself in the story and Susan's father in the magic." —*The Booklist*

"The ending makes *Time at the Top* unique."
—*The Horn Book*

"Recommended."—*Bulletin of the Center for Children's Books*

TIME AT THE TOP

Edward Ormondroyd

Illustrations by Peggie Bach

BANTAM BOOKS
TORONTO · NEW YORK · LONDON · SYDNEY

This low-priced Bantam Book
has been completely reset in a type face
designed for easy reading, and was printed
from new plates. It contains the complete
text of the original hard-cover edition.
NOT ONE WORD HAS BEEN OMITTED.

RL 5, IL age 9 and up

TIME AT THE TOP

A Bantam Book / published by arrangement with
Parnassus/Houghton Mifflin Company

PRINTING HISTORY

Parnassus Press/Houghton Mifflin edition published August 1963
8 printings through January 1981
Bantam edition / June 1982

ISBN 0-553-20960-4

Published simultaneously in the United States and Canada

PRINTED IN THE UNITED STATES OF AMERICA

0 9 8 7 6 5 4 3 2 1

for
Kitt and Beth

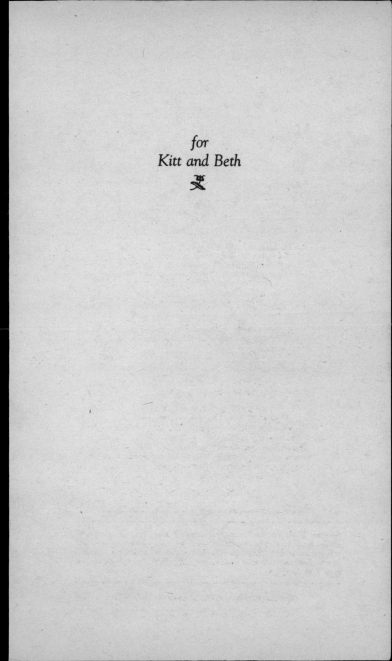

🦌 1 · WHAT BECAME OF SUSAN? 🦌

One Wednesday in March, late in the afternoon, Susan Shaw vanished from the Ward Street apartment house in which she lived with her father.

The last person to see her was Mrs. Clutchett, a lady of uncertain age but reliable habits, who was employed as a cleaning woman by various residents of the building, and also by Mr. Shaw as a cook. Wednesday was her day to clean as well as cook for the Shaws, so she had been in the apartment when Susan arrived home from school—an arrival, she thought, that was a little later than usual. She reported that Susan had behaved in a moody and restless manner, as if the weather, which was certainly unpleasant enough, had gotten into her bones. The girl fidgeted about the apartment for a while "without a word to say for herself," suddenly muttered something about "going to the top," and went out. According to Mrs. Clutchett, that took place some time after five o'clock, although she wouldn't swear to the exact moment. "The top," no doubt, was the seventh floor, the topmost one of the apartment building, where Susan sometimes went to look out of a window at the end of the hallway.

Mrs. Clutchett had, however, just glanced at the clock when Mr. Shaw walked in, so she could state with authority that his arrival took place at fourteen minutes to six. He was carrying a beautifully wrapped box, and called out as he entered, "Here you are, chick—the loudest one in the whole store!" Mrs. Clutchett gave a small shriek at this announcement, having immediately concluded that the box contained something explosive. Mr. Shaw assured her that it was only an alarm clock for Susan, and asked where she was. He was told of Susan's presumable whereabouts, and sat down to read the paper. Dinner was ready at six-ten. At six-thirty, Mr. Shaw, more irritated than alarmed, took the elevator to the seventh floor to fetch Susan down. She was nowhere to be found.

I first heard of the disappearance around eight o'clock that night, when Mrs. Clutchett breathlessly telephoned me to ask if I'd seen Susan.

"Susan who?" I asked.

"Susan-Shaw-on-the-third-floor. You know, the little girl of that nice Mr. Shaw, with the braids and brown eyes?"

"Oh, yes," I said. I didn't really know Susan, but we had ridden the elevator together once or twice. "What's the trouble?"

"She's *gone*, poor motherless lamb! She's just disappeared into thin air!"

"Oh, she's probably at a movie. I always watched movies two times through when I was her age, to make sure I got my money's worth."

"No sir! That child *never* goes out without leaving a note or saying what she's up to. I wish I could think it was just a movie, but I can't. There's something going on here, Mr. Ormondroyd. You just mark my words. There's something behind all this."

I had to smile. Mrs. Clutchett cleaned my apartment

every other Thursday, and I had come to know her as a curious compound of sentimentality and devotion to mystery. She loved to see in almost everything that happened a huge and sinister plot, suspected by no one but herself. Nearly anyone you could name was probably "up to something" that would astonish the world "if only truth were told." I could see her now at the other end of the line, pursing her lips and nodding with that air she had of ominous satisfaction.

"Oh, nonsense," I said. "She's probably visiting one of her friends."

"Well! I just wish I could think so. I just hope to goodness it's that simple. Poor Mr. Shaw's telephoning all her friends now, and I'm calling all the people in the building—but it won't do any good. We'll have to bring in the police, I can just feel it in my bones. Poor child! It's just those kind that have something awful happen to them."

"Well, I'll have a look around up here," I said. "If I see her I'll send her right home."

"That's awfully nice of you, Mr. Ormondroyd. But I've got a hunch it won't do any good. There's more than meets the eye here, *you mark my words*." And with that dark utterance she hung up.

I did take a look up and down the hallway of the fifth floor, where I live; but Mrs. Clutchett was right to this extent, that it didn't do any good. There was no Susan in sight.

Next afternoon, Thursday, Mrs. Clutchett boarded the elevator as I was going down.

"Did it turn out all right?" I asked.

"No *sir!*" she said in sorrowful triumph. "What did I tell you! Didn't I say there was something behind all this? That poor child has vanished without a trace!"

"Oh oh!"

"Yes indeed, you may well say 'oh oh!' You'd probably have cause to say more than that if truth were told. Now, I'll tell you what," she said, lowering her voice dramatically and fixing me with her eye. "This whole thing could've been prevented, if you ask me. Nipped right in the bud."

"Really? How?"

"Well, now! It's not that he isn't a good father to her—maybe *too* good, trying to make it up for her, you know. Lucky for him she's so stage-struck that she doesn't think to plague him for things like most girls plague their fathers, because I know he couldn't deny her anything. But if I've told him once, I've told him a hundred times, 'Mr. Shaw,' I've said, 'you ought to marry again. A good-looking, steady man like you. It's not right for the poor child not to have a mother, girls need the influence of a good woman,' I said. Not that I don't respect his feeling. I know what it's like, believe you me. Why, when poor Mr. Clutchett was taken to Heaven I made a vow right then and there never to *look* at another man again, to keep his dear memory ever green, so to speak, and I've kept that vow through thick and thin, believe me, not but what there weren't strong temptations to break it. But *I* didn't have chick nor child like Mr. Shaw has, and that makes a difference, you can't deny it, feelings or not."

"So you think she ran away because of not having a mother?"

"Well, now," she said, changing her tack as if suddenly realizing that such a simple reason didn't have many possibilities for mystification. "I just hope to goodness that it's nothing worse. Not that I'm reproaching him with it now, you understand. Poor man, he's half frantic with worry. I'm staying by his side through thick and thin. I'm just going out now to get some coffee, he's drinking it by the gallon, won't eat a bite. No, I won't say another word about it now, but just you wait till that child comes back, *if* she comes back, won't I just lay into him *then*, night and day, until he finds a good respectable woman to marry and give that poor child a home!"

I went with her to buy coffee. She talked nonstop all the way to the store and all the way back, veering between real concern and delighted foreboding. The police had been notified and were working on the case under the direction of a certain Detective Haugen. They had searched the building from basement to roof, and had gone over the elevator with magnifying glasses and finger-print equipment, without result. Susan's picture and description had been sent out through the city and to other cities nearby: Missing, Susan Shaw; age, height, weight, etcetera etcetera; wearing a dark coat, grey and red pleated wool tartan skirt, grey pullover sweater, white socks, saddle shoes; reward for information leading to recovery. There were several theories to account for what had happened. She might have run away, she might have amnesia, she might have been kidnapped. Poor Mr. Shaw was still arguing hopefully against all three possibilities. There was no reason, he said, for Susie to run away—she was doing well in school, he had never quarreled with her, she seemed happy enough for a motherless girl. Amnesia wasn't likely; you had to suffer severe strain or shock to lose your memory, and although the death of Mrs. Shaw two years ago had been a terrible blow, nevertheless Susan had come through it very well. And as for kidnapping, what could kidnappers hope to gain by taking such a risk? He was not rich; he was only an accountant with a very small company, and his savings amounted to nothing that the most desperate of abductors would consider worth while.

It was simply a scandal, Mrs. Clutchett went on, the way the tenants were behaving. Well, some of them, anyhow—pretending they had business on the third floor just so's they could walk by the Shaw's apartment and stare in the door. Still, it had to be admitted that most of the people in the building were being just as kind as they could be, offering to cook or run errands, or bringing sandwiches to try to tempt poor Mr. Shaw into eating something to keep his spirits up. Even Mr. Bodoni, the janitor, had come up and had actually (for the first time in his life, probably) taken that horrible dead cigar out of his mouth and put it in his pocket as a sign of respect. He had patted Mr. Shaw on the shoulder, steered him into the kitchen, and whispered solemnly, "You show me anyting here it's outa repair, *any*ting, I fix it right now. No questions asked. Right now—everyting else can wait." Later he came in again with an enormous bunch of daffodils, and, removing his cigar once more, expanded his offer: "You show me anyting here, it don't even *have* to be outa repair, I fix it. All brand-new parts."

"Now wasn't that real sweet?" Mrs. Clutchett said moistly. "It just goes to show you, doesn't it? I'd never have thought it of him in a hundred years—him being foreignborn and usually so mysterious in his ways and all."

"Is there anything I can do?" I asked.

"Well, Mr. Ormondroyd, if you're a praying man as I sincerely hope you are, *most* writers I fear being the contrary, then I guess you better get down on your knees. Police and detectives and all irregardless, I've got a hunch we'll never see that poor child again without Heaven's help. You just mark my words."

☙ 2 · HUBBUB IN THE HALLWAY ☙

The mystery unexpectedly deepened late Thursday night.

Detective Haugen, who suspected that they were dealing with a kidnapping, had stationed a policeman in the Shaw's apartment in case an attempt should be made during the night to deliver a ransom note. At about one-twenty-five A.M. the policeman heard what he thought was a child crying in the hallway. He rushed out to investigate, and found a large black tomcat nervously sniffing the carpet and yowling. On the floor lay a scrap of newspaper with writing on it. 'Ransom note!' he thought; 'Haugen was right!' He wrapped a handkerchief around his fingers, and was stooping to pick up the note when he noticed that the elevator was ascending. (The elevator was on the opposite side of the hallway from the Shaw's apartment, and one door down.) The indicator arrow above the elevator door was steadily creeping around the dial. It had just reached 4 when he looked. He raced into the Shaw's apartment and telephoned the precinct station. "Get hold of Haugen!" he shouted. "I think we've got 'em. They may be going up the elevator right now. —That's right, I said *up.*—That's what the arrow said. —Look, don't argue, get Haugen and some of the boys here, quick. We've got to cut 'em off!"

The building was quickly encircled and all exits covered by armed policemen. Searching parties swept through the building, working their way upward floor by floor—one group up the inside stairs, two up the outside fire escapes.

Nothing. The elevator stood empty on the seventh floor.

"Up to the roof, boys," Detective Haugen ordered. "Don't fire unless they do first. Keep your eye on the hallway here, Murphy."

Nothing!

It suddenly occurred to Detective Haugen as he huddled against the wind on the roof that perhaps the elevator business had been a ruse. You didn't have to be *in* an elevator to send it anywhere. You could press the button from outside. Perhaps the kidnappers had sent the elevator up to divert attention, while they walked or ran downstairs. They might have been able to leave the building before the police arrived to surround it—or they might have gone on to the basement to hide out until the excitement blew over . . .

"Come on, boys!"

No one was in the basement.

However, on a dusty part of the floor they found a cat's pawmark. And behind the row of washing machines, by a puddle that had formed there from a leak in one of the hose connections, were several muddy footprints.

"Those weren't here last time we searched," Detective Haugen said. "Look, not even dry yet. Go up and get one of the girl's shoes, Murphy."

The footprints were slightly larger than Susan's shoe. Nevertheless, they were much too small to have been made by an adult.

Since the basement was Mr. Bodoni's particular province, he was seized for questioning as he entered the building a few minutes later. Had he been down in the basement recently?

"Yeah," said Mr. Bodoni.

When?

"Bout half an hour ago, three-quarters of an hour, along in there, I guess."

Had he seen or heard anything out of the ordinary?

Mr. Bodoni looked at the ground and shifted his cigar evasively.

Well?

"Don't tell the tenants, willya?" Mr. Bodoni muttered. "Everyting's under control. I only seen one."

"One *what?*" Detective Haugen shouted. "Out with it, man!"

Mr. Bodoni leaned forward and hoarsely whispered, "Mice!"

Coming home from a late movie, he had entered the elevator and found a mouse in it. He had been fighting mice for three years, and had finally reached the point where he could look any tenant in the eye and say there wasn't a mouse in the house. And now this! He put his foot on the creature, descended to the basement, where he had seen and heard nothing unusual, and collected his mousetraps. Needing bait, he had gone out to an all-night delicatessen for some cheese, and had been grabbed by two policemen on his return. "Whatsa matter?" he demanded. "A man can't buy cheese any more? It's against the law to buy cheese? Buyin' cheese, at's all I was—"

"Okay, okay," Detective Haugen sighed. "Forget it."

"That black cat upstairs yours?" Murphy asked.

"What cat? No cats around here. I use traps, see?" He produced one from his pocket. "Don't say nothin' to the tenants, willya? I get everyting under control before they notice."

The piece of newspaper that had been found in the hallway was not a ransom note. The pencilled writing on it said:

> *Dear Daddy, please don't worry about me. I'm all right. Tell the policeman he can go away, I'm all right. I have to go back for a little while but please don't worry, it's perfectly safe. I'll be home as soon as I can.*
>
> *Love, Susie*

"Careful, Mr. Shaw, don't touch it—there may be fingerprints."

"That's her writing, all right!" Mr. Shaw said. "I'd recognize it anywhere. See that loop on the a's? Thank God she's safe!"

"Well, Mr. Shaw, I don't want to alarm you, but this may be a trick of some kind. They could have forced her to write it, see? 'Tell the policeman he can go away'—that sounds like a fabrication to me. One thing, anyway; if they're clumsy enough to try something like that they're clumsy enough to get caught."

"At least she's safe," Mr. Shaw insisted. "She says she's safe."

"I hope so, Mr. Shaw."

One faint, dusty fingerprint was found on the paper, and identified as Susan's.

※

I went to the Shaws' apartment Friday afternoon to see if I could be of any service. Mrs. Clutchett told me of the previous night's happenings—she had been sleeping in the apartment on the living room sofa—and introduced me to Susan's father. He looked worn, but hopeful.

"She says she's safe," he said, showing me her note. "I

believe her. See how steady the writing is? If anybody had forced her to write it she'd be frightened, and the writing would show it, wouldn't it? But it doesn't even waver. She *must* be all right . . ."

Meanwhile Mrs. Clutchett was making mysterious signals to me behind Mr. Shaw's back—so mysterious, in fact, that it took me several minutes to interpret them as meaning "Come into the kitchen." I reassured Mr. Shaw as well as I could, pointing out that the last sentence in Susan's note struck me as particularly encouraging, and then followed Mrs. Clutchett into the kitchen.

"Look!" she whispered dramatically, pointing under the sink.

I looked. All I could see was a black cat crouching over a dish of hamburger and making little gargled *rowr rowr* noises as it ate.

"So?" I said.

"If—that—cat—could—talk!" she said, pursing her lips and narrowing her eyes in an expression of vast significance. "Well! Believe you me, that animal's in the thick of this. I've just got a hunch. I'm keeping my eye on it night and day."

"Oh, great!" I said. "Well, when kitty decides to reveal all, just let me know. I'll be right down."

"All right! All right! You go ahead and laugh if it so pleases you. But just you let me tell you something. I used to have a cat, and you may believe this or not but it's the pure gospel—*one month to the day* before poor Mr. Clutchett was taken to Heaven that cat cried for twenty-four hours without stopping. Now! *Cats know.* You mark my words."

The cat, however, kept whatever secrets it might have had, and Friday night passed without incident.

On Saturday morning a number of people happened to converge on the Shaws' apartment at the same time. Detective Haugen had come to report that nothing had changed, but that his bureau was following up a lead anonymously telephoned in from New Jersey. With him came a young reporter carrying a camera, and a man bearing flowers who was later identified as the vice-president of Mr. Shaw's company. At the same time, four tenants, two men and two women, all acquaintances of Mr. Shaw, approached down the hall from the opposite direction. As everyone arrived simultaneously at the door, it opened to reveal Mr. Shaw and Mrs. Clutchett in the midst of an argument just within. He was insisting that she must go home and get some rest, not that he didn't appreciate her concern; and she was saying that not even wild horses could budge her an inch until that poor child was found. Behind them was the night-guard policeman, stretching and yawning. For a few minutes there was a subdued hubbub at the door, with everyone murmuring "Excuse me. Pardon me." Detective Haugen glanced impatiently at his watch. It was eight-twenty-three.

At that instant the elevator door opened with a sigh, and Susan got out.

She had an odd dress on: it was black, with full-length sleeves, a good deal of material bunched and draped around the hips, and skirts that reached halfway between her ankle and knee. She was also wearing black cotton stockings, and shoes of a strange cut. There were bits of straw in her hair. She was limping, and had dark circles under her eyes. Still, most of the startled observers later agreed that her expression was one of happy excitement; but Mrs. Clutchett immediately diagnosed it as a combination of shock and hysteria.

Mr. Shaw turned pale, and murmured "Susie, Susie!" as she flung herself at him. Mrs. Clutchett shrieked. Instantly there was an enormous uproar. "Susie, Susie! Are you all right, darling? You're not hurt?" "Oh, Daddy, I'm *awfully* sorry if I made you worry. I didn't mean—" "Now, Miss,

where did they leave you? What did they look like?" "Hey—smile! That's it!"—and the glare of a flashbulb. "Those clothes!" the women murmured to each other. "Where do you suppose she got those *clothes?*" Doors began flying open up and down the hallway. "Now leave the poor child alone," Mrs. Clutchett shouted, "can't you see she's *exhausted?*" Within the apartment the cat yowled. "Hold it"—flash!—"one more, now!" "What kind of car did they have? Where did they let you off? Where did that straw come from?"

Susan fainted.

"Now you've done it!" Mrs. Clutchett shrieked. "Get out, get out, all of you! *Hounding* the poor child!" She seized a cushion from the sofa and began laying about her violently, while Mr. Shaw carried Susan inside. "Out! Out! I never heard of such a thing! That child says nothing and sees nobody until she'd had a rest and some broth and a doctor. Get *out!* Big grown ignoramuses pestering the poor baby to her death!"

As soon as she had been laid on the bed, Susan opened her eyes and giggled. "Wasn't that a perfect faint? I had to get rid of all those people somehow. Oh, Daddy, you look so tired! I'm awfully sorry if you worried. Did you get my note? No, I *didn't* run away. No, I wasn't kidnapped either. Well, I was going to explain the other night, but there was a policeman—"

"The idea! The idea!" Mrs. Clutchett raged into the bedroom. "Those—those *vultures!* Chafe her wrists, Mr. Shaw. Where's my smelling salts? I'm going to call a doctor."

"No you're not," Susan said. "I'm perfectly all right. I just sprained my ankle a little, that's all. Now please go away, I want to—"

The cat yowled under the bed.

"It's Toby!" She wriggled off the bed and dropped on

her knees. "Come on, Toby. Puss puss! I'm awfully glad you're not lost. I promised them I'd bring you back. Daddy! You'll *never* guess how old Toby is, and he doesn't even know it! He's sixty, plus—what's eighty-one from a hundred?"

"Back on that bed, Missy! You're overwrought, that's what you are. Sixty my foot! Although I just *knew* that cat was in the thick of it somewhere. Just wait till I see that Mr. Ormondroyd, thinks he's so smart—"

"Puh-lease, Mrs. Clutchett! I have to talk to Daddy in private. Will you please, please, kindly—"

"All right, all right! I'll go and make some broth. But if you ask *me*, a doctor should—"

"And please shut the door? Please? Thank you."

"Susan Shaw," said her father, clutching his hair with both hands and pulling it, "*will* you please tell me what's been going on around here?"

"Of course, Daddy, I'm going to. Come on, Toby, that's a good boy. Well, it all began—when was it?—Wednesday. That horrible day, remember? Oh, I bet you're not going to believe a word of it, it's all so—so *weird*! But cross my heart and hope to die, it's all absolutely true!"

⚛ 3 · A DAY AWRY ⚛

Wednesday went wrong from the very beginning.

Susan was awakened by a burst of wind that seemed to be trying to rip her bedroom window right out of its frame. Evidently it was going to be another foul March day, the third in a row now, with bitter air, a sunless sky, and an unresting grit-and-paper-bearing wind. She groaned, pulled the blankets up to her chin, and glanced at the clock.

It was seven. She had slept through the alarm again.

"Oh, no!" she muttered, flinging herself out of bed. There still might be time to dress and get out of her room before—but no, she was too late. The television set next door burst into noise. Even the wind couldn't drown out that dreaded greeting. "Yap yap!" shouted Your Genial Breakfast Host, "yap yap yap!" on a soaring note of jollity; and then a crash of applause and whistles and glad cries. Susan huddled her clothes on, trying to deafen at least one ear by pressing it against her shoulder. "No, serious-ly," the Genial Host shrieked through the wall into her other ear, "isn't life the funniest thing you ever heard of in your *life?*" Laughter, clapping, cries. She slammed her bedroom door behind her.

Mr. Shaw was standing by the window in the living room, looking down at the street as he knotted his tie. "Sounds like they beat you to it again," he grinned.

"Oh," Susan groaned, "I can't *stand* it. My fault for sleeping through the alarm again, I guess . . . Can I have a new one, Daddy?"

"Alarm clock? Sure, chick. What color would you like?"

"Oh, I don't care. Just so it's loud. All this one says is tinkle tinkle."

"One—loud—alarm—clock," said Mr. Shaw, writing in his notebook, "color no object. Done. Meanwhile, since it's an ill wind that blows nobody good, etcetera etcetera, maybe our friends' antenna will get carried off. Listen to it!"

"Wish it would carry old Yammerface off." Imitating the Genial Host, she cried in a high-pitched voice, "Yap yap a funny thing happened to me on the way to the studio this morning yap yap the wind blew me right into the middle of last week!"

Breakfast was a fiasco. Mr. Shaw started out by spilling coffee on his trousers. While he was changing, the toaster stuck and thoroughly carbonized the two slices of bread in it. Susan burned her thumb trying to pry them out. The second toast-making attempt was more successful, but as she was buttering a slice it slipped from her fingers and fell butter-side down on her skirt. She kicked the table leg, and went to change. Every skirt but the tiresome grey and red tartan was out at the cleaners. "No, seriously," the Genial Host yelled on the other side of the wall, "are you good folks having fun?" Roar. She fled in her slip, and changed in the living room.

The wind was increasing. They picked at their toast without appetite.

"Well," Mr. Shaw sighed at last, looking at his watch, "it's about that time."

"Yes."

"What's the matter, chick?"

"Oh . . . I have a feeling it's going to be one of those days."

"I *know* it's going to be one of those days. Still, life goes on."

Reaching the sidewalk, they were nearly knocked down by a gust of wind, and as they kissed each other goodbye a sheet of newspaper flew at their heads and wrapped its wings about them like some demented seabird. Mr. Shaw went up Ward Street to the subway, while Susan went two blocks in the opposite direction to catch her bus to school. When she reached the bus stop she discovered that she had no money—it was still in the pocket of her buttered skirt. She had to go back for it, thereby missing the bus and arriving late at school.

There was in her grade a small, leering, unwashed boy who had appointed himself her official tormentor. With proper vigilance she could usually avoid his attentions; but during the first period the class was seated in alphabetical order, which placed him directly behind her. Today, in her preoccupation, she forgot to take the normal defensive steps. Almost instantly her braids were in the hands of the enemy. It cost her a painful wrench of the neck to jerk free. She rounded on him and hissed, *"Stop that!"*

"Susan!" said Miss Melcher.

"But he was—"

"Do pay attention, Susan!"

"Well, I'm trying to, but he keeps—"

"You must try a little harder, Susan."

'All right, you little rat,' she raged to herself, 'just wait till I catch you!' She endured his pestering until the bell rang, then managed to trap him at the door, where she kicked his shin. Miss Melcher looked up just in time to see it.

"Susan Shaw," she said in her high sorrowful voice, "Susan Shaw, why can't you Adjust?"

The Physical Education teacher bellowed, "Doesn't this lovely wind just make you want to shout, girls?" Shivering and sniffling, they were herded out into the elements. A soccer ball came soaring out of the boys' side of the playground and hit Susan on the ear.

She struggled through a particularly difficult set of arithmetic problems, discovering only after she was finished that she had been working on the wrong assignment.

The cafeteria ran out of Swiss steak just as she arrived; she had to take frankfurters, which she loathed.

Her enemy pressed close to her as they entered the first afternoon class. He did not look at her. His face expressed only eagerness to reach his desk and begin his work. She allowed herself to relax. He let fly a backward kick, caught her thwack on the kneecap, and darted out of range. The Problems of Modern Living teacher was staring out the window at the time.

But classes came to an end at last, and Susan's spirits rose as she hurried toward the auditorium for the Thespian Club meeting. Now the whole dismal day would be set right! Yesterday tryouts had been held for "The Lady and the General: a drama of Revolutionary Boston," and she had been at her best. Today Miss Melcher would assign the parts. There was no doubt in Susan's mind who would get what. She was smiling as she took her seat.

Miss Melcher saved the plum until last. "For Lavinia, the feminine lead, Elsie Mautner," she said, avoiding Susan's eyes; and the day's ruin was complete.

Susan boarded the homeward bus and collapsed on her seat in bitterness and despair. "Acting is my *life*!" she frequently told her classmates. At the age of nine she had been a fairy in the neighborhood Little Theatre performance of "A Midsummer-Night's Dream," and she had

gone on the stage at every opportunity since. She had a
flair for thinking herself into a role, and making an audience believe her in it. Furthermore, she had the quick
wit that is so necessary when things go wrong. Last year,
for instance, she had twice saved the Thespian Club play
with her ad-libbing; once when the Chambermaid had
burst into hysterical giggles instead of saying, "The King
approaches!" and again when the wicked Duke had somehow gotten himself locked in the toilet and missed his
entrance cue by half a minute. She loved costumes of all
kinds, particularly long, full-skirted dresses that whisper
when you walk in them and flare out so beautifully when
you make a quick turn. That was the kind of dress this
year's lead would have, and Susan had had her heart set
on playing the role. Lavinia, a Boston Belle: the part
wasn't very well written, but it had possibilities nevertheless; possibilities that Elsie Mautner wouldn't be able to
see even if you wrote out a description of them in words of
one syllable.

She, Susan, had been assigned the part of a Towns-
woman, with only one appearance in the first act—"Enter
Townspeople, left,"—where all that was required of her
was to gape at the British soldiers as they marched off to
Bunker Hill. When she had complained after the meeting,
Miss Melcher said, "Of course, Susan, you did beautifully
last year. But, you see, it's very important to let everyone
Participate, isn't it?"

"Yes, but it's more important to do the play *right*,"
Susan argued. "The parts should go to the people that can
handle them best, shouldn't they? That's all I—"

"Now, Susan. We must learn to Fit In With The Group.
We can't all be prima donnas all the time, can we?"

That was unjust. Susan had no false modesty about her
talent, but she was no prima donna. It was just that if they
were going to the trouble of putting on a play at all, they

should do it as well as possible. It wasn't right for Miss Melcher to regard the play as a Social Experience rather than as an artistic problem; and it wasn't right that Lavinia, a Boston Belle, should be played like a dressmaker's dummy, which was what Elsie would make of the part. And Susan knew, she just *knew*, that the minute something went wrong—and something would go wrong, it always did— Elsie Mautner would freeze up and fumble her lines; while she, Susan, would quietly die in the wings, because she couldn't stand to see anyone, even Elsie Mautner, make a fool of herself in front of an audience . . .

"Oh, go argue with City Hall!" she muttered savagely as the bus stopped at Ward Street. "Elsie *Mautner!*" Flinging herself down the step, she caught a button in the folding door and tore her coat sleeve.

❧ 4 · GIFT OF THREE ❧

"Little girl! Little girl! Yoohoo!"

There was nothing Susan detested more than being called "little girl." Perhaps she was slightly smaller than average, but she was one year ahead of her age group in school; and most of the time she certainly *felt* more mature than anyone seemed willing to give her credit for. 'I'll pretend I don't hear,' she thought, wrinkling her nose. 'Maybe it's not for me, anyway.'

She was on Ward Street, one block from home. Bursts of wind still drove between the buildings, and the clouds that scudded just above the rooftops looked too wet to be able to stay aloft much longer. It was the rush hour. Tension was in the air, as bitter to the taste as the exhaust fumes that swirled over the sidewalks. There was a traffic tie-up at every corner. Above the clamor of the horns Susan could hear the voices of a cabbie and a truck driver inviting each other to "just step out in the street and say that again, wise guy!"

"Yoohoo! Little girl!"

'No,' Susan thought, quickening her pace. But then curiosity got the better of her and she turned.

A strange sight! An old woman, so enveloped in flapping loose ends of clothing that she looked like a dark wind-whipped flame. Her arms were full of unidentifiable objects. She nodded down the street, crying plaintively, "Little girl! My hat!" And certainly there was something— Susan could not recognize it at that distance and in that light as a hat—being harried along the sidewalk by the wind.

'Little girl!' Susan snorted to herself; but the old woman looked so helpless that she repented, and called out, "All right, all right!" and self-consciously set out in pursuit.

It was uncanny how agile the hat was. It dodged between people's legs and shot out from under their hands as they stooped, and twice it actually leaped into the air to escape her clutch. Everyone on the block seemed to be gaping or grinning at her as she hurried along. Her face felt as though it must be glowing like neon. 'Hope it blows into the street and gets smashed by a ten ton truck,' she thought furiously. But just at the corner the wind failed for a moment, and with a great leap she had the thing trapped under her foot.

It was made of green plush, and covered with broken plumes and scraps of fur and glass beads and paper roses and little tucks of chiffon. It was dusty without and greasy within, and smelled of cheap pomade.

Susan picked it up distastefully by the end of one plume, and trudged back up-wind again. She was not eager to meet the owner. Her one glimpse in the failing light had given her the impression that the old woman was one of those crones with safety pins stuck in their ruined coats and packets of newspaper in their pockets, who wander about the city streets mumbling to themselves and poking in trash cans. They are hard to face when you are warmly dressed and well-fed. But she was wrong. This woman was not one of those. And yet what an extraordinary creature she was! She had on a shawl and a muffler and three overcoats, one on top of another, and numerous skirts and underskirts and petticoats. Each garment was a different color, each was loose and ill-fastened, and all were making violent efforts to go the way the hat had gone. Her withered hands were encrusted with dime-store bracelets and rings. Her hair was henna-rinsed, and streamed out in loose ends like the thatches that sparrows build behind drainpipes. Her face was covered with white powder, rouge, eye-shadow, lipstick; but everything was slightly askew: one cheek spot was higher than the other, her eyebrows had different slants, her mouth was smeared at the corners.

But her eyes were bright as a lizard's.

"Thank you, dearie," she crooned. "So sweet. Children are so unmannerly these days, usually. Oops, my shawl! Nasty weather. Nicky'll be along in just a minute. Oh dear! Oh my!"

She had been making efforts to shift her burdens, which included an umbrella, a newspaper, and a bulging paper bag. Now as her momentarily free hand clutched her hat, the bag tipped over and discharged a quantity of potatoes.

"Oh my! Contrary things. Help me, dearie, I can't bend over. Lumbago."

The potatoes seemed infected with the same passion for freedom that the hat had shown. They rolled into the gutter and under the feet of the passersby, while Susan scrambled about on her hands and knees after them. The old woman struggled with the wind and her clothes, saying, "Oh my, oh dear, oops" in a quavering, plaintive tone. And when Susan had finally gotten most of the potatoes together, and stood up with her arms full of them, and two clamped under her chin, the old woman's umbrella said *Flump*!! and blew inside out right in her face. Of course she dropped the potatoes again, and the bag ripped open and spilled more. Susan muttered a word that only fathers should use. But the old woman just said, "Hurry, dearie, Nicky's coming," so down on her knees she had to go once more.

"Put the spuds in my shawl, dearie. That's it. Oops, mind the muffler." That ravelled length of wool had taken a dislike to Susan, and was flogging her face unmercifully. But this time she kept her hold on the potatoes. The old woman beat the muffler down and got it under control; but meanwhile part of the newspaper saw its chance for escape, and seized it, and went flapping and disintegrating down-wind.

"Oh dear. Well, don't mind it, dearie, all lies anyway, I expect. Just so long as I've got the want ads."

Somehow everything was clawed, clutched or crammed into order again. The potatoes were bundled up in the shawl, the rebellious muffler defeated for good and tucked under the collar of the second overcoat, the shattered umbrella turned right side out and furled with most of its ribs in place.

"Thank you, dearie. *So* sweet. Now then, I'll give you three. No more!"

"Beg pardon?" said Susan.

"Ooh, there's Nicky! Yoohoo! Right over here, dearie!"

A powerful motorcycle had appeared at the curb. Its rider was dressed in black from head to foot—black boots, black pants, black leather jacket and gauntlets and helmet. The upper half of his face was covered by immense goggles, while the lower half was either lost in shadow or covered with a dense and closely-cropped beard. The old woman hopped briskly on the pillion saddle. "Just three!" she called back, and her cut-glass rings winked as she held up three skinny claws. Then the wind caught her unawares again, the motorcycle blasted away into the traffic, and they rapidly vanished from sight, leaving a wake of bouncing potatoes and newspaper sheets and blue smoke.

"Well!" said Susan. Everything had happened so quickly that only now could she sort out what had been a series of confused impressions and sights and sounds; but, sorting them, she saw how queer it had all been.

'Three?' she wondered, crossing the street to her own block. 'Three what? Potatoes? But she didn't actually hold them out to me or anything. Maybe I was supposed to pick them up when she dropped them from the motorcycle. No, that couldn't be it. Oh, wasn't she a marvellous type! If I ever have to be a crazy woman in a play, I'll try to look just like her—all those clothes and that weird make-up. Funny, the wind never stopped where she was. And that umbrella. Sort of like Mary Poppins. "Just three," she said. Awfully queer. Like a fairy story—oh no! *Oh no!*'

Three!

Three wishes?

'Susan Shaw,' she said fiercely in her mind, 'don't be stupid!' But she stopped walking in spite of herself, and her heart tightened. The whole episode had been just strange enough . . .

She had loved fairy stories in her younger years. But how irritated she had always been at the people in those stories who were granted three wishes only to make a mess of everything! In those days such things still seemed to be within the realm of possibility, so she had decided how she would proceed if it ever happened to her. It was very simple and logical. On the first wish she would ask for something small and harmless, just to make sure she really had the power. Then, very quickly, before she could think of something silly and spoil it all, she would wish that she might never make mistakes, or ask for anything that could get out of control. And then on the third wish she would wish that she could have an unlimited number of wishes. And then—!

"It's all nonsense," she whispered. "I wish—" She looked

quickly about her. Her face was hot with shame at her silliness; but her heart thudded with impossible hope. "I wish," she mumbled into the wind for her first, or testing, wish, "I wish there was a ring—let's see, make it a gold ring with a small emerald—in my coat pocket."

Her trembling hands crept into her pockets.

There was no ring.

"I *told* you!" she muttered savagely, "Gosh, what a—oh, honestly, Susan Shaw, they ought to put you in a mental institution!"

It was just the sort of trick you could expect of a day like this. As if she hadn't had sufficient warning from everything else that had happened!

※

Mrs. Clutchett was dusting when she entered the apartment.

"Well, there she is, home from school. How the day flies! Susie, you should've worn a warmer coat, you could catch your death in this wind. Why, child, what's the matter?"

"Oh, nothing."

"Here, now, you just let me fix you a nice hot cup of cocoa. There's nothing like—"

"*No!*"

"Well, I'm sure!"

"Oh, I'm sorry, Mrs. Clutchett. I mean, no thank you. Really I'm sorry. It's just been such an awful day."

"Hasn't it, though! I never saw such weather. It's those atom bombs, you mark my words. We never had such days when I was a girl, believe me. And you with nothing on your legs and a skimpy little coat! Now, Missy, you sit by the radiator. I'm going to fix some hot cocoa, and you're going to drink it. Catching your death! Talk about awful days," she continued from the kitchen, "don't tell me! If my vacuum cleaner didn't go on the fritz *three times*! That Mr. Bodoni stuck his screwdriver in it to see what was the matter, and didn't pull the plug first, and almost got electrocuted and blew the fuse. I don't know about that man. Those slow ones are awfully deep sometimes, you never know what they're really up to. Not that I need the vacuum cleaner here. It's like taking money from a baby to clean here, you keep it so neat. Not like some I could name. You take Mr. Ormondroyd—socks on the floor, shirts on the floor, cigarette ash—you wouldn't believe it! Keeps his papers locked up, though, oh yes, tight as a drum, you can't even get a peek at them. I wonder if he isn't up to something. Writers! Mr. Clutchett knew a writer once, this fellow *claimed* he was a writer, *but*—well, you may believe this or not, but it's the gospel: *that man was a counterfeiter.* Yes sir. They came and took him away one fine day. Twenty-dollar bills, that's what *he* wrote."

The cocoa had a skin on it.

Mrs. Clutchett resumed her work, still talking. As soon as her back was turned Susan poured the cocoa into the rubber-plant pot; cocoa skin made her stomach turn. Mrs. Clutchett rattled on unheeded. Susan kicked her legs back and forth and chewed her knuckle. After a while she tried the television set. Nothing but commercials; toothpaste, breakfast food, scouring powder, smiles, smiles, smiles. She turned it off. The evening paper was on the sofa. She flopped on the floor and began to leaf through it from back to front. The funnies weren't funny—why did she read them any more? The astrology column told her to take her time and to be on the lookout for a great opportunity—'such as three wishes?' she thought, loathing herself. The Hollywood column had an article about her favorite star, a beautiful woman whose roles of courage, nobility and self-sacrifice always left Susan with a lump in her throat. The star was getting her fourth divorce under lurid circumstances. "Citizens Should Support Proposed Bond Issue," said the editorial. She sighed and turned to the front page.

FORTUNE FOUND AT CONSTRUCTION SITE

There was a map, with the caption "Thar's Gold In That Thar Playground, Podner!" Why, she knew the place. It was a few blocks up Ward, around the corner, and down a side street. Her mother used to take her there. Oak Park, everyone had called it, although it was only a small square of asphalt without a tree in sight. With a flicker of interest she read:

> "Gold!"
>
> The heart-stirring cry of Sutter's Mill and the Yukon was heard here today as construction workers unearthed a fortune in old U.S. coins in a condemned playground.
>
> The lucky finder was Frank M. Zalewski, 27, a bulldozer operator employed by the Delta-Schirmerhorn Construction Company. The company is erecting a 12-story office building on the 93rd Street site (see map).
>
> "The 'dozer blade lifted it out," Zalewski said. "It was only about a foot under. I saw all this stuff shining in the dirt, and then everybody started hollering 'Gold!'"
>
> The treasure consists of $60,000 in "eagles," or $10 gold pieces. The coins all date from 1863 or earlier. It is believed that the owner may have been killed in the Civil War and thus was unable to reclaim his buried hoard.
>
> Martin Van Tromp, numismatics ex-
> *See Page 4, Col. 7*

The trouble with treasure, she thought, stifling a yawn, was that it was always found by someone else. Any other news?

MAYOR ASKS BOND ISSUE FOR WATER

A burst of sleet rattled against the window. Oh foo! It was too hot in here. She tossed the paper aside, stood up, stretched, and said, "I'm going to the top."

As she pressed the elevator button the thought came to her again: 'What did the old woman mean by three? Three *what*?'

⚜ 5 · THE ELEVATOR ⚜ MISBEHAVES

That elevator always reminded me of a tired old horse. It groaned when it started and groaned when it stopped. It labored up or down the shaft at such a plodding gait that you wondered if you were ever going to arrive. The door sighed when it opened or shut. I once suggested to Mr. Bodoni that we should either put the poor thing out to pasture or have it shot. "Yeah," he said, not getting the joke but willing to be amiable about it.

Around the top of the inside walls was a little frieze of cast-metal rosettes and curlicues. Mr. Bodoni, inspired one year by both the Spring weather and a sudden urge to express himself, had begun to paint these red. I don't know which gave out first, his paint or his inspiration; at any rate he stopped halfway through the fourteenth rosette, and has not finished the job to this day. The rest of the inside was painted buff.

There was the usual bank of buttons—ten of them, including the basement stop, the emergency stop, and the alarm—and a dial-and-arrow above the door to show which floor you were approaching. A yellow ticket assured any-

one who wanted to read it that the mechanism had been
inspected and found satisfactory by a Mr. Scrawl Blot
Scribble, who I sincerely hope is a better inspector than
he is a penman. Mr. Bodoni had also hung up a ticket,
with *No Smokking in Elvater, Please!* thickly pencilled there-
on. (His own cigar was always dead, and didn't count, of
course.) Finally there was a metal plate which said *Capacity 1500 Lbs.* I remember that when I first met Susan she
was staring at this, moving her lips and ticking off her
fingers.

"How does it come out?" I asked.

"I can't make it come out right," she said. "If everybody
weighed a hundred and fifty pounds you could get ten
people in, but what if they all weighed two hundred
pounds? I'm not very good at arithmetic."

"Hmm," I said, and I began to work on it too. But I'm
not very good at arithmetic either, and she had gotten off
at her floor before I arrived at an answer.

Going up the elevator now, Susan occupied her mind
with the usual arithmetical speculations.

'Fifteen hundred ulbs,' she thought. "Or is it libs? Almost
a ton. Or is a ton one thousand? No, two thousand.
Suppose everybody weighed a hundred and seventy-five.
Let's see, one seventy-five into . . . um. I wish Mr.
Bodoni'd learn to spell. One seventy-five into fifteen hundred, make it nine, nine times five is . . . um. At least
Elsie Mautner's even dumber than I am in arithmetic. Try
eight. Eight fives are forty, that's a zero, maybe it'll come
out even, let's see, carry the four . . . um. Wonder how
many people *do* weigh a hundred seventy-five? Pretty heavy.
Oh well, almost at the top. I'll work it out on the way
down.' For the arrow was creeping past six. Too bad there

weren't arrows in the classrooms at school to save you when you were stuck on a problem . . . The arrow plodded up to seven and stopped.

The elevator kept on going.

It was the strangest sensation—as if the elevator were forcing its way up through something sticky in the shaft, like molasses or chewing gum. There was a thin humming noise all around her, and the light dimmed. She was startled, and a little frightened. But of course there were only seven floors, so the elevator would have to stop at the seventh. The arrow must be out of order. She would have to tell Mr. Bodoni. He'd look mournful, the way he always did when something went wrong, as if it were all your fault.

Now the elevator stopped. The door said "Sighhh . . ." and opened. Susan clutched her hands together and said, "Oh!"

'They must be redecorating,' she thought in astonishment. 'No, that can't be it; you don't redecorate a hallway. Maybe it's a private suite? But why should the public elevator open into a—?'

It was a hallway she was looking into, but it certainly wasn't the seventh-floor hallway of the apartment building as she remembered it. For one thing, the floor, instead of being covered with brown carpeting, was bare parqueted wood, beautifully polished. For another thing, there were no numbered doors opposite; the wall there was solidly wainscotted with oak. Against it stood a marble-topped table with carved lyre-shaped legs, on which were a vase of paper flowers and a stuffed owl under a glass bell. Everything was glowing with—was it sunlight? Sunlight on a March evening like this?

She became aware of sounds. There must be a clock nearby, and a large one too: tock—tock—tock—a stately sound. A bird was singing; not a canary, something richer

and wilder and much more inventive. And wait a minute—
yes—no—chickens? Impossible! And another sound; a
serene whispering murmur, rising and dying. It could only
be one thing, a breeze rustling through foliage. And yet
only a few minutes ago, downstairs in the apartment, she
had heard the rattling gusts of March against the window.

The scent of flowers was very strong.

She stepped out of the elevator in a daze. Yes, there was
a clock, a grandfather one, with hunting scenes painted
on its porcelain face. The sunlight came through a window to the right of the elevator. It was a funny kind of
window, very tall and narrow, with two sets of curtains:
straight-hanging white lace framed by drawn-back red velvet. It was open; all the strange scents and sounds were
coming through it with the sunlight, irresistibly drawing her
to investigate. She leaned her elbows on the sill and
stared out, filling her lungs with warm sweet air and
murmuring, "Oh my." She had never been any closer to
the country than the seaside resort in New Jersey where
her father took her during summer vacation. But this was
countryside, all right: she could just tell, even though all
she could see was a portion of hedged-in garden. The
hedge was a tall tangle of roses and privet and honeysuckle. Hydrangeas grew under the window, lifting their
pale blue pompons to the sill. The grass was badly in need
of cutting, and had flowers growing in it. The base of one
of the huge trees on the lawn was encircled by a white-
painted iron settee.

'I'm dreaming, that's all there is to it,' she thought. 'I've
fallen asleep over the newspaper. It's like *Alice in Wonder-
land*. I'll probably try to get into the garden, but the door
will be too small, or the golden key will be lost, or
something, and there'll be a little bottle with a label
saying "Drink Me," and a White Rabbit—no, it's a black
cat.' For a large black tom had emerged from the hedge,

and was plowing nose-first through the grass like a ship through waves. The bird abruptly ceased its singing, and began to scold: "Mew! Mew!" 'A bird mewing like a cat?' she wondered. 'Maybe the cat sings like a bird . . . Oh well, pretty soon Mrs. Clutchett'll poke me with her broom and say, "C'mon, Susie, help me set the table." '

"Maw-w-w-!" said a cow in the distance; and she wondered why she should dream that. 'Very realistic of me,' she thought.

The elevator door sighed, and trundled shut.

"No, wait!" she gasped. "*Ow!*" Springing back from the window, she cracked her head against the sash. Her eyes filled with tears. She wasn't dreaming—no dream could hurt like that. Through the blur she saw that the elevator was gone. There was no door in the wall. Solid, unbroken wood paneling!

'Oh no, oh no!' she thought in a panic, searching for the button.

"Vicky!" a woman's voice called. "Vicky?"

Someone was coming. There was no button on the wall, and not enough time to recall the elevator anyhow. But she had no business being here! Quick! Where? The red curtains! She slipped behind the nearest one, and squeezed herself as thin as she could. Fortunately they reached all the way to the floor.

The footsteps came down the hallway, and with them a curious rustling sound as of long skirts. She could not resist a quick peek. What she saw made her catch her breath. It was a lovely, tall, slender woman with masses of rich chestnut hair piled on her head. Susan, always susceptible to beautiful ladies, felt her heart go out to this one at once: 'That's what I want to be like when I grow up,' she thought. And the woman must be an actress, too. Why else would she be in costume? She had on a grey dress whose skirt came down to the floor; it had a lot of material draped around the hips, but was tightly fitted from the waist up. All she needed was make-up to be ready to step out before the footlights.

"Vicky?" she called again, stopping by the grandfather clock.

"What's the matter, Mama?" Now a girl came running down the hallway from the opposite direction. She was slightly taller than Susan; her hair was a dark coppery brown, and fell in waves below her shoulders. She wore a dress similar to her mother's except that the skirt was shorter, and black cotton stockings.

"I just heard the strangest noise somewhere around here!" said the woman in a puzzled voice. "Did you hear anything?"

"No, I was talking with Maggie. What kind of noise?"

"Well, it's hard to say—a kind of rumble, I think it was, and then a thump . . ."

"Oh, I expect it was just Toby. Shall I look for him?"

"No, I don't think . . . it sounded like something rolling or sliding. And then a very distinct thump, like— oh, like a bird flying against the window."

"It must have been Toby, chasing that catbird—they hate each other so."

"I suppose you're right . . . Well, I'm sorry I disturbed you for nothing."

"Oh, *Mama*. Maggie says supper is almost ready anyway. Doesn't the honeysuckle smell just glorious?"

"Mm, lovely."

They moved off down the hallway with their arms about each other.

"Mama, everything outside is getting so jungly. Why don't we have a gardener in?"

"Well, dear," Susan thought the woman's voice was a little evasive, "suppose we wait just a bit longer. Mr. Branscomb is coming tomorrow afternoon about the investments, and after he's gone I'll think about it . . ." Their voices faded down the end of the hall.

'Well, that's funny,' Susan thought. 'I never saw either of them before. If they lived up here I would have seen them in the elevator.' It had come to her that part of the seventh floor must have been converted into a very realistic stage set, and that the woman and the girl had been rehearsing their parts in a play. But no, that couldn't be it. No stage set that she had ever seen was so realistic that you could hear cows and smell flowers and feel the warmth of sunlight. And if this were the seventh floor of the apartment building, *why hadn't the woman recognized the sound of the elevator?* That rumbling sigh was unmistakable after you'd heard it once . . . Well, it was all very queer. Even as a dream it would have been the strangest she'd ever had.

She crept out from behind the curtain and began to look for the button again. If that elevator could come up here once—wherever "here" was—it could come up again. But there was no button. And while she was still peering and poking helplessly along the wainscotting she heard the sound of running feet approaching. This time she lost her head. She darted toward the window curtains, changed her mind and stepped back, glanced desperately about for a better hiding place, and at last, without a second to spare, threw her leg over the windowsill and dropped down the other side—falling through the hydrangeas with a tremendous thrashing and crackling. 'Good grief, what a racket!' she thought; 'Like an *elephant!* I hope the bushes cover me.'

Apparently they did, for the girl's voice said, right over her, "All right, you naughty Toby cat! Breaking the bushes! Just wait till I catch you, that's all! And if I don't, Bobbie will tomorrow, and then see if you don't regret the day you were born!"

'Now I've really done it,' Susan sighed when Vicky had gone. 'Although I suppose I could go to the front door and say, "Pardon me, but there's an elevator in your house that you don't know about, and I have to use it." No, no—all that explaining . . . It's hard enough to explain when you know *what* you're explaining. I certainly don't have any idea of what this is all about. Well, I'll just have to wait till it's dark, and sneak in, and try to get that darned elevator up somehow. Poor Daddy'll worry when I don't show up for dinner. And Mrs. Clutchett will be snorting around and making things worse . . . How am I ever going to explain this to *any*body without making them think I've gone absolutely insane . . . ?'

She might as well make herself comfortable for the wait. She snuggled down in the litter of dry leaves, murmuring, "What a day! What a stupid impossible crazy

day! I should've stuffed my ears with cotton and gone back to bed and stayed there this morning." Wrapped in blankets, impervious to noise—the idea began to make her feel drowsy. The air was as warm as her own bedclothes; the stirring bushes lulled and hushed, more comfortable to the ear even than silence. 'It *is* a dream, really,' she thought, yawning. 'I hope I can remember it to tell Daddy . . .'

6 · THE MEANING OF THREE

It was dark when she awakened. 'They've let me sleep through dinner,' she thought. Why should they do that? "Daddy?" she said. There was no answer. Something crackled under her as she shifted.

Then she remembered. It wasn't a dream after all.

She crawled out from under the hydrangeas as quietly as she could, and stood up on the lawn, and then caught her breath with wonder. The sky was ablaze with stars. Where had they all come from? She had never seen more than a few score, feebly competing with the city's neon; here they were beyond imagining in number. 'Why, that must be the Milky Way,' she thought, recognizing that glowing swath overhead from a picture in one of her science textbooks. And in gazing up at it she discovered something else that the city would never have let her find out. The night sky could be *heard*. It was like the sound of the sea in a shell, only much fainter, as though it had come to her straining ears from as far away as the dimmest star.

There were other sounds too. The grass was full of crickets, who were chirping and rustling as they moved about through the stems, so that the whole lawn whispered with them. She was sure she heard frogs nearby. And suddenly in the distance a train said, "Way a *wayyy* oh-h-h-h-h," sweet crescendo, sad diminuendo.

'If I lived here,' she thought, 'I'd never go to bed, never. I'd just sit outside all night and look and listen . . .'

But she simply had to go back: her father would be worried sick by now, and furious with her for making him worry. All the windows of the house were dark. It was a very large house, she noticed now, tall and narrow and with a profile reminiscent of a castle. She would just have to hope that everyone was asleep, and that she could find an unlocked door. Slowly she began to grope her way through the shadows.

'Wish there was more moon,' she thought after five minutes of blundering. 'There seem to be hedges all over the place. Ouch! Thorns. Well, here's an opening. That sounds like frogs—must be a pond nearby.'

She was right. At the next step there was no ground under her foot; she sprawled forward clutching at the air, and *slosh!*—she was under. Fortunately the water was only waist-deep, and she was on her feet again immediately. The bottom was squdgy. Something cold and soft slithered across her bare knees. She shuddered, and scrambled up the stone bank.

"They'll all be ruined," she muttered, taking off her clothes and wringing them out. "Stupid place for a pond!" But she didn't want to stand about naked while they dried, so she put them on again. They clung to her, and her shoes squelched with every step. It was a good thing that the weather was so warm. What if it had been March here too? The very memory of the wind and sleet she had left behind—how long ago now?—made her shiver.

In another ten minutes she was clear of the hedges and shrubbery, and had found a flight of wooden stairs against the dark bulk of the house. She crept up them one step at a time, testing each tread for squeaks; and thank goodness! there was a door at the top, with a handle that turned easily and quietly.

'Now,' she thought, standing in the interior darkness, 'which side of the house am I on? I'm all mixed up. This might even be the wrong floor . . . I know, I'll listen for the grandfather clock. It was near the elevator.'

Room after room, all caves of shadow; windows that pretended to be doorways; doors that hid themselves in the darkest corners; sharp-cornered furniture everywhere. She groped along inch by inch, hardly daring to put her hands out for fear of knocking something over, and wincing at every move for fear of striking her face against some unseen projection. She could not hear the clock anywhere.

Eventually she found herself at the foot of a staircase. She felt her way across the bottom stair; encountered the newel post, all knobby with carving; felt her way around that, and met a table top; put her hand on something cold that gave under her touch; and *crash!*—the sound of a metal object bouncing on the floor. Not very loud, actually, but loud enough.

She crouched, suffocating.

A door opened softly upstairs. Pause. Then a whisper: "Toby!"

Pause.

"Toby?"

"Meow!" said Susan, with all the realism she could muster.

A long heart-pounding silence; then the upstairs door softly closed again.

She remained motionless for a few more minutes, to make sure that all was quiet above, then straightened up. Suddenly, somewhere to her left, a sweet melancholy chime struck the quarter hour.

'There it is!' she thought, sagging with relief. As quickly

as the dark permitted she went toward the sound, discovered a doorway, and—yes! it was the hallway, all right. Up ahead was the dim patch of light that must be the window, and beyond it she heard the clock solemnly knocking each passing second on the head with its pendulum.

'Now for the button—there *must* be a button.'

She began to run her fingers over the wainscotting. There was no button. The wood seemed to be glowing somehow. Brighter and brighter—her shadow loomed and wavered on the paneling—

She whirled around.

There stood Vicky in a nightgown, holding a trembling candle aloft and staring at her round-eyed with fright. She seemed on the verge of screaming.

Susan hissed, "Now don't yell or do anything silly! I'm not a ghost."

"Are-are you a burglar's accomplice?" Vicky faltered.

"Of course not. I'm just lost, that's all. Soon as I can find the elevator I'll go away. Do you know where the button is?"

Vicky stepped backward. "Button? What button?"

"The *elevator* button. Oh, I forgot—you don't know about the elevator, do you? Look, I know it doesn't make any sense, but I'm not crazy, really. Why do you keep staring at me like that?"

"Your *clothes*."

"Well, what's the matter with them? They're just wet, that's all. I fell in your pond."

"It's not the wet . . ."

"What's the matter with you?" Susan burst out after a moment's silence. "You act like I was a freak or something!"

"It's your clothes," said Vicky. "They're the oddest I ever saw."

"Well, that nightgown of yours is pretty hilarious, too,"

Susan retorted. "And what about those dresses you and your mother were wearing this afternoon? I never saw such funny old-fashioned clothes in all my life."

"Why, they are *not* old-fashioned! Mama just bought that dress a month ago!"

"You mean for a play? Is she going to be in a play?"

"No, of course not—just to wear. Don't you know what people wear?"

"Certainly I know what people wear!" Susan said in exasperation. "And I know perfectly well that people don't wear clothes like that any more. In the Gay Nineties, maybe, but not in 1960."

The other girl retreated a step, and the candle shook violently in her hand. "I think you're mad. I didn't say anything about 1960. I mean right now. This year."

"What do you mean, this year?" said Susan, beginning to feel a bit frightened. "I'm *talking* about this year. It's 1960."

Vicky shook her head.

"Well then, for goodness sake, what year *is* it?"

"Don't you really know? It's 1881, of course."

"Oh!" Susan gasped. The shape of the house! The design of the dresses! The funny curtains by the window! All the oddities she had noticed in the last few hours clicked into place in her mind. "Eighteen—eighteen—oh no! What's happened? Where am I? What street are we on?"

"Street? It's not a street, it's a country road."

"All right, all right, but what's it called?"

"Ward Lane."

Well, that sounded right—or almost right. "But where's the city?"

"Don't you know? It's about five miles from here."

"Five *miles!*" Susan moaned, clutching her head. "Oh, am I lost! Am I ever lost! Listen—when I got on the elevator I was *in* the city, on Ward *Street*, and it was 1960!"

"Nonsense," Vicky said faintly. "Things like that can't happen."

"I know they can't! Look, I don't want to argue: I just want to go back. I'm here whether it can happen or n—" Striking herself dramatically at the word *here*, she felt something hard in the pocket of her skirt. "Look!" she continued excitedly, "I can prove it—about being from the twentieth century, I mean. You know about dimes and quarters, don't you? Well, here, look at the dates. Oh, go on, take them, I'm not going to hurt you!"

Vicky hesitantly took the coins and held them close to the candle flame. "What funny designs they have! Oh! This one says 1953! 1945! 1960—oh, my goodness! 1960! You—maybe you are from the twentieth century. But it's impos—how could you possibly *get* here?"

"I've been *telling* you, I came in the elevator. Do you know what an elevator is?"

"We may live in the country," Vicky said, "but we are not backward."

"All right, I'm sorry. I didn't know whether they'd been invented yet. Anyway, I got on this elevator where I live, just across the hall, and it let me out here instead of where I thought I was going, and then it went down again and I can't call it back. You know, I'm beginning to think the stupid thing wants me to be here."

Vicky gave a sudden start. "*Wants* you to be here?"

"Oh, I know it sounds silly—it is silly. I just can't think why—"

"No," Vicky whispered. "No. It isn't silly." Her eyes were widening again, and the candle in her hand shook so

much that it almost guttered out. "I just remembered
something. The well! It must be the—yes, it has to be! *It
worked!* Look, you don't have to go back right away, do
you?"

"Well, I ought—"

"Look," Vicky interrupted with growing excitement,
catching Susan by the sleeve, "you *can't* go back now, I
simply must talk with you. Really, it's *essential.* Come up
to my—are you hungry? I'll get something to eat. And we'll
have to get those wet clothes off you. Oh, my heavens,
talk about—! I was right, I was right—it's perfectly true,
Maggie doesn't know what she's talking about! Here, wait,
don't move a step, I'll be right back!"

She hurried soundlessly down the hallway, and returned
in a minute carrying some slices of bread and a pot of jam.

"All I could find in a hurry, I'm afraid. Maggie's hidden
everything because Bobbie's coming home tomorrow, and
he always— Come on, you *must* tell me all about it, and
I'll tell you about—oh, it's just unbelievable!—please be
very careful on the stair, we mustn't wake Mama up."

Susan, utterly bewildered, allowed herself to be led on
tiptoe up the stairs and cautiously along a second-floor
hallway.

"Oh, what a lovely bed!" she exclaimed on entering
Vicky's room. It was a high four-poster with a frilly arched
canopy, and curtains at the head.

"Ssshh! You mustn't talk loud. Mama's a fairly sound
sleeper, but Maggie has ears like an owl. Yes, isn't it a
beauty? Grandmama left it to me in her will. Here, you
can wear one of my nightgowns. Take off those wet
things—I won't look. I'll put some jam on the bread. Oh
pooh, I forgot the spoon. I guess we can just dip the slices
in. Wish we had some tea. Does the nightgown fit all
right? I'm a little taller than you."

"Yes, it's fine. Where shall I put my things?"

"Oh, over the back of the chair is all right, they'll dry soon. That's awfully nice material. What funny shoes! Does everybody wear such short skirts in the twentieth century?"

"Yes, why not?"

"It seems so immodest. But I suppose if everybody does it's all right. I don't wear corsets myself, neither does Mama. She says they're such a torture, and there's no sense in it if your waist is naturally slender. Thank goodness ours are! Here, sit on the bed, you can put your feet under the sheets if they're cold. Oh! My manners—you must forgive me, I'm so excited about the magic. I don't care if it *does* sound silly, it *is* magic. I'm Victoria Albertine Walker."

"Susan Shaw."

" 'Charmed to meet you, Miss Shaw. Isn't the weather delightful?' That's what we say in Deportment Class," she giggled. "Now! Please tell me what happened, and don't leave out *any*thing, because it may be of great importance."

So Susan recounted the events of the day. When she got to the part about the old woman with the runaway hat, Victoria's eyes grew rounder and rounder, and she hugged her knees; and as soon as the tale was finished she burst out:

"Yes, of course! The old woman was a witch, a good witch!"

"A witch?" Susan said. "That's craz—" She checked herself. Everything else was crazy—why not a witch? "She didn't look like one, anyway. I thought she might have been a gypsy or something."

"Of course she didn't look like one. They never do, that's just the point. If she looked like a witch you'd do whatever she asked, to get her blessings, and it wouldn't be any test of your character. You see? It's like that in lots of stories. But if they look like someone else, and they're troublesome, and you help them out of the kindness of your heart anyway, then they know that you're worthy."

"Hmm. Well, that could be it, I suppose. But I still can't figure out what she meant by giving me three. Three what?"

"Why, that's perfectly plain. They always give you three of something. She must have meant that you could have three trips in the elevator to here!"

"Ohhhh! That could be it, couldn't it? But why here?"

Victoria gave her a long speculative look. "That's what I wanted to talk to you about. I think I know why."

"Why? How can you know?"

"Because—oh, it's all so spooky! *You were sent here on purpose because I wished you here.*"

Susan felt a shiver race down her back. "Me? How did you know about me?"

"Oh, I didn't wish for you in particular; just—somebody." She hesitated a moment. "Cross your heart and hope to die you won't tell? It's a *very serious* secret."

"Cross my heart three times and hope to die."

"All right. Well, first I wished on a star. You know, 'Star light, star bright, first star I see tonight.' Do you do that in the twentieth century too? Anyway, it didn't work. Then I remembered there was an old abandoned well about half a mile down the lane, and I thought, 'Maybe it's a wishing well.' So I asked Maggie, she's Irish, but she said no it wasn't, that was all blasphemy, only God can grant your wishes and He doesn't do it very often because it's not for the good of your soul. And she believes in ghosts, too, can you imagine? But I don't care, it can't be blasphemy if you're wishing for someone else's sake—can it? So I went there this very afternoon, and I threw in the thing I love best, a little gold locket that Papa gave me when I was ten, and I marched around it three times, and I said, 'I wish someone would come and chase Mr. Sweeney away.' "

"And?"

"Well, I never dreamed it would happen this way—but here you are!" Victoria concluded triumphantly.

"Oh, now, wait a minute!" Susan protested. "I can't—who's Mr. Sweeney?"

"Oh, he's this perfectly dreadful man who's been absolutely hounding poor Mama to marry him."

"Oh! Is your father—?"

"Yes, poor Papa died two years ago."

"Why, so did my mother."

"Oh, I *am* sorry . . ."

"Anyway," Victoria went on after an interval of silence, "I was hoping some handsome man with a noble brow would come along, and show Mr. Sweeney up for a scoundrel and give him a thrashing. But I'm sure you'll do just as well. You're from the future, after all, you must know an awful lot. Oh no," she added hastily, seeing that Susan was going to interrupt, "I don't mean *you* should thrash him. Maybe you could just—I don't know. Scare him away, maybe."

"Well, I don't know . . . Why doesn't your Mama turn him down?"

"Oh, she has. But he's so persistent. He's after her money, I'm certain of it, the scoundrel. Poor Papa left quite a lot . . . Sweeeeeeney," she drawled in a savage falsetto. "Isn't that a dreadful name? I couldn't stand having a name like that."

"Why, your Mama could marry anyone she wanted to," Susan said warmly. "She's the most beautiful lady I ever saw. She's as beautiful as a movie star!"

"Oh, how poetic! 'Beautiful as a moving star.' I'll have to write that in my diary. Yes, she is. But, you know, she's been so—oh, resigned since Papa died. She sold our city house and buried herself out here because Papa loved it here so much, and she won't go out in society where she could meet suitable men. And Mr. Sweeney keeps lurking around and forcing his attentions on her and wearing her down, until I'm afraid she'll say yes just to have some peace . . . Well! We won't have to worry about it until tomorrow. My brother Bobbie's coming home from school tomorrow. We'll have to consult him first anyway, he's the man of the house now, even if he's only twelve. Robert Lincoln Walker. Don't ever call him Bobolink, it makes him furious."

"Oh, I can't stay till tomorrow. I have to go back."

"But Susan, you only have three trips, it's a shame to waste one."

"Yes, but my father is probably frantic by now."

"That's right, I forgot . . . But look, it's so late; surely a few more minutes won't matter?"

"Well . . . just a few."

"Good! Tell me about your Mama. You don't mind talking about it?"

So Susan told her all she could remember. Then Victoria told Susan all about her late Papa. Devouring bread and jam by candlelight, they agreed that two parents seemed to be able to take care of themselves, but that one alone required careful management; which was a great responsibility, but no doubt worth it in the long run. Then Victoria swore Susan to secrecy, and brought out her diary, and read selected parts of it out loud; which proved so fascinating that Susan resolved to keep one of her own as soon as she could begin. (Although she determined that *her* style would be more brisk, and would not run so much to sad pure thoughts, and moonlight on marble gravestones, and noble breaking hearts and so on.) And of course certain passages in the diary brought them around to the subject of Boys; and Susan quite forgot about going home while they pursued that fascinating topic . . . Gradually their voices began to trail off—they yawned—the silences grew longer; and at last the two friends slept, curled up on the bed, while the candle burned down to a puddle of wax and put itself out.

⚔ 7 · HATCHING THE PLOT ⚔

When Susan awoke the next morning she found a note on the night stand, propped against the candlestick:

Dear Susan—Don't make a sound. No one suspects.
I'm going to smuggle some breakfast up for you. I'll
knock 3—2—1. If anyone tries to enter without the
secret signal hide under the bed. Isn't it all romantic?

> *Victoria*

It certainly was, she thought, smiling and hugging herself. It was like living in a stage setting for one of those period plays she loved so much. 'Marvelous props!' she thought, looking around her with a professional eye. But no, she had to force herself to realize that these things weren't here to convince an audience. People lived with them and used them every day. They were *real*; the tall spindle-backed rocking chair, the footstool with its carved legs and quilted upholstering, the secretary with its little drawers and cubbyholes and scroll-surrounded top shelf, the tall chest of drawers surmounted by a kind of miniature balustrade, the marble-topped dressing table on knobbed legs. Best of all was the bed. Although the room was

warm, she wriggled under the sheets to savor the luxury of being in a four-poster. Tall walnut columns, dark green velvet canopy, curtains drawn back at the head—why didn't they make beds like this any more? They were so much beddier than modern ones. You felt like someone in a piece of furniture like this . . .

Then her conscience had to spoil it all.

'Better be going back,' it said.

'No, I won't go back for a while,' she answered defiantly. 'I'd just have to explain and explain, and nobody'll believe me. Why should they, I don't really believe it myself.'

'That's no excuse. The longer you stay, the more you'll have to explain.'

'I don't want to go to school,' Susan pleaded. 'Elsie Mautner will just be impossible, going around with her head all swelled up and sort of smiling at me whenever we meet. Thinks she's so wonderful! She can't even act in a crowd scene without looking like a wooden post. Bet if *she* were thrown into 1881 she'd have hysterics.'

'That's no excuse either. Your father's worrying, and you know it.'

Her heart squirmed within her. 'Poor Daddy . . . Oh, go away!' she raged. 'He doesn't *have* to worry, I'm perfectly safe. It isn't as if I'd had an accident or something.'

But she could no longer enjoy the four-poster. She got out, splashed her face in the washstand basin, and went to the window. The front lawn was below, an immense overgrown space containing circular flower beds and a pair of iron stags. Then came a privet hedge, very shaggy, and a wrought iron gate; then a dirt road on the other side; and beyond that, open fields starred with daisies and Queen Anne's lace; and then woods.

'I can't get over how sweet it smells,' she thought, pushing her conscience aside and breathing deeply. 'That

must be Ward—what did she call it?—Ward Lane. Ward
Lane, Ward Street, same thing . . . ? Oh! I know what
happened—no, wait, it hasn't happened yet, it *will* happen. The city's going to grow out here, there's plenty of
time for it; sixty years plus eighty-one from a hundred is
. . . um. Lots of time, anyway, cities grow so fast. And
then Ward Lane turns into Ward *Street*! I bet the apartment building will be built right on this spot! And that's
where the florist will be, and the five-and-dime; and
Benjamin's Men's and Boys' Wear will be right by that tree
. . . And none of the people that run them or shop in
them are even born yet. Why, come to think of it, *I'm* not
even born yet!' That was such a weird thought, and it
gave her such a spooky feeling, that she murmured:

"Weird Street—that's what it really should be called."

There was a quiet knock at the door, three, two, one,
and Victoria slipped in.

"Oh, you're up! Good morning, isn't it beautiful out?
That Maggie! She has eyes like a hawk. Bobbie steals food
all the time, it's second nature for her to keep her eyes on
the larder. So this is all I could get," producing from her
pockets two hard-boiled eggs and a muffin sliced in half
and filled with jam. "Don't worry, when Bobbie's here
we'll feed you better, he's an expert. 'Foraging raids,' he
calls it: he wants to be a soldier. We're perfectly safe for a
while, Mama's writing letters in the sun parlor. Oh, we'll
have to hide your clothes. You can wear some of mine,
just in case somebody sees us. You are staying just a little
longer, aren't you?"

'No!' said Susan's conscience.

"Well . . ." Susan said.

"You really must, you know," Victoria said. "It's a
responsibility. I've thought it all out. You can't accept a
piece of magic one minute and turn it down the next
without *serious* consequences."

'So there!' Susan told her conscience. "All right," she said, "I'll stay for a little while, anyway."

"Good! You *are* a dear! Now, Bobbie's coming this afternoon right after lunch, the trap'll drive him in from the station. Then we can all think about chasing Mr. Sweeney away. Now please don't frown so, Susan, there's a dear. That's what you're here *for*, you know. I'm sure we'll think of something. Well! we don't have to worry about it until this afternoon, anyway. The main thing right now is clothes. Here, tell me which dress you'd like."

So the problem of Mr. Sweeney was dismissed for the time being; and Susan spent a fascinating morning trying on all of Victoria's dresses, one after the other, in front of a gilt-framed oval mirror, while Victoria fussed around her with the pleasurable little frown of a fashion expert.

Robert arrived—not in a trap, as Victoria had predicted, but on foot—at one o'clock in the afternoon. Very shortly thereafter, while the reunited Walkers were still talking and laughing downstairs, Susan saw a horse and buggy coming up Ward Lane. It stopped at the gate. A tall, thin man got out, threw the reins over the gatepost, picked up a dispatch case from the seat, and started up the walk. Susan dodged behind the curtains just in time to avoid being seen by him as he glanced up at the house. She wondered if it could be Mr. Sweeney. If so, why should Victoria have such an aversion to him? As far as she could see, he was quite distinguished looking.

His arrival set off another burst of talk below. But soon there was quiet again; then footsteps in the upper hallway, and whispering just outside the door, of which Susan caught three words, "Now behave yourself!" And then Victoria entered with an owlish-faced, rather plump boy. He was dressed in a short-trousered suit, black stockings, and high shoes.

"May I present my brother Robert?" Victoria said in her Deportment Class voice. "This is Miss Susan Shaw, Robert."

"Pleased to meet you," Robert said dubiously.

"Pleased to meet *you*."

They shook hands.

"Isn't the weather delightful?" Susan said desperately after a while.

"I guess so."

"Oh, for goodness sake, Bobbie, stop staring!" Victoria burst out. "Where are your manners, anyway?"

"Well, gosh, Vic, I never saw anybody from the twentieth century before. She doesn't look any different to me. I think you're just telling me a big story."

"Of course she doesn't look any different, why should she? She has my clothes on, not hers. Show him the coins, Susan."

Susan brought them out and handed them over.

"Great Caesar!" Robert said. "1960, 1945, 1953! They certainly *look* real . . ." He stared at Susan again. "But say, there can't be an elevator by the clock, you know. The wall's too thin."

"Well, that's where I got out," Susan said. "Really."

"But it's only a foot thick!"

"Well, I can't help that. You can watch when I go down again, if you don't believe it."

"Well," he conceded, "maybe it sort of bulges the wall on the outside of the house . . . Hey, do they—?"

"Don't say 'hey,' " Victoria broke in. "It isn't at all nice."

"Oh, sisters!" he groaned, making a comic face at Susan. "Always ragging at a fellow! Do they still have soldiers in the twentieth century?"

"I'm afraid so."

"That's good. I'm going to be a colonel by 1910, I've got it all worked out. Hey, Vic, guess what! You know who drove me from the station?"

"Jim Perkins?"

"No—Mr. Sweeney! And you know what he said?"

Victoria pressed her hands to her breast and sank into a chair. "Oh no!" she said. "Don't tell me he—you mean you *accepted a ride* from him?"

"Well, what could I do? Jim wasn't there."

"I can just imagine he wasn't. No doubt Mr. Sweeney saw to *that*. Getting you into his clutches! I thought we agreed that we would not have anything to do with him beyond ordinary politeness. Didn't we?"

"I know we did, Vic, but listen! I don't think we've been fair. He's really all right once you get to know him. Really! You know what he said? He said that if him and Mama—"

"*He* and Mama," she interrupted automatically.

"He said that if he and Mama get—uh—"

"Oh, it's all right," she sighed. "Susan knows the situation. All right, what's the wonderful thing that happens if he and Mama, perish the thought, do get married?"

"He said if they do, he's going to send me to military school!"

"Oh," said Victoria icily. "Now he's an angel. Now he's all right, really, once you get to know him. Of course he's just doing it out of the kindness of his heart! *You* don't have to do anything for *him*, I suppose! *Do* you, Robert dear!"

"Well," Robert said, coloring, "I guess he did mention

that it wouldn't hurt if I put in a good word for him when I saw Mama."

"And were you going to?"

"Well, my goodness, Vic! I haven't said anything to her *yet,* have I?"

"Oh, Robert Lincoln Walker, you are the despair of my life!"

"Well, thunderation!" he burst out. "Women just don't understand. I don't know why I don't run away and join the army right now, and work my way up through the ranks! You might take me seriously then. Mama thinks I'm still in *curls,* and you treat me like a six-year-old. Rag, rag, rag! At least Mr. Sweeney knows what a fellow feels. He knows how to treat a fellow. He let me drive his mare two miles, and he gave me a puff of his cigar!"

"He *what?*"

"There! See? That's just what I mean! You don't think a fellow *ever* grows up. What am I supposed to do, wait till I'm *eighty* for my first cigar?"

"Oh, Vicky," Susan broke in soothingly, "don't look so shocked. It isn't fatal. How did it taste?" she asked Robert.

"Well . . . I guess I coughed a little. But a fellow could get used to it if he tried. And besides," rounding on Victoria again, "I'll bet Papa would have let me do the same, if I'd asked him. Hey, Vic. Hey, wait a minute, don't cry."

"What Papa would have done," she sniffled, "and what Mr. Sweeney does are as different as night and day. Don't you *dare* disgrace P-P-Papa's memory by comparing them."

"I'm sorry, Vic, honest. I didn't mean—I guess I got riled."

"Here's a hanky," said Susan helplessly.

Victoria hiccupped once or twice and dried her eyes.

"Thank you, Sue, I'm all right now. I'm sorry if I ragged you, Bobbie. I know you're growing up, really I do. But you ought to be grown up enough to see what Mr. Sweeney's trying to do: he's trying to worm his way into your good graces. It's all very well for you to think he's a fine fellow and to fall for his flattery, but don't you see?—it's *Mama* who will have to marry him. It's Mama we're really talking about, not you."

"Well, why doesn't she send him packing, then?" Robert said sulkily.

"You know very well she's tried. But he'll *never* give up as long as he thinks he has a chance of getting her money. You know that that's all he wants, don't you?"

"You can't prove it."

"*Prove* it! I don't have to prove it, I know it. All you have to do is look at him to know he's a fortune hunter."

"He looks all right to me."

"Oh, what do boys know about these things? Of course he looks all right to you—he makes a special effort to. He wouldn't get very far if he looked like a scoundrel, would he? Listen! Did you ever see him alone when he thought no one was looking?"

"No."

"Well, I did. You know what he did? He looked at everything—the room and the furniture and the rugs and the curtains and the pictures—he simply *devoured* everything with his eyes; and all the time he kept rubbing his hands together. Rub, rub, rub . . ." As Victoria spoke she mimicked what she had seen. Susan was fascinated. What an actress this girl might have been! Her imitation of gloating greed was as convincing and chilling as the real thing. "And *that*," said Victoria, "is what you want Mama to marry, is it?"

"Well—"

"Rub, rub, rub . . . ?"

"All right, all *right*. But what can *we* do about it? Listen, you never gave me a chance to tell you. You know the *real* reason why he drove me home? He didn't just drop me and go back to town. He's going to board at the Hollisters'. He says he's going to lay siege to Mama, and he won't let up till he's carried the fort!"

"Ahh!" said Victoria slowly. She shot a significant look at Susan. "So—he's right next door. This is our chance, Sue!"

"Oh, that isn't Mr. Sweeney downstairs?" Susan said.

"Goodness, no—that's Mr. Branscomb. *He's* a gentleman."

"He's the lawyer who handles Mama's money," Robert added. "Hey, Vic, what do you mean, this is your chance? What have you two got up your sleeve?"

"Oh, it's just this crazy idea Vicky has," Susan said uneasily. "I don't—"

"It isn't a crazy idea," Victoria said. "We just have to go through with it, now that the witch and the well have gone to all the trouble of bringing you here."

"Well?" Robert asked. "What well? What is all this mystery, anyway?"

"I didn't tell you everything, there wasn't time," Victoria said; and she proceeded to explain the part that she thought the wishing well had played in Susan's arrival.

"You mean," Robert said when she finished, "that Susan was *sent* here to chase Mr. Sweeney off? That's a major campaign! How are you going to do it, Sue?"

"I haven't the faintest idea," Susan said helplessly. "Listen, just because I'm from the twentieth century doesn't mean that I can do *any*thing. I'm still just a girl, not a—a *genie* or something."

"We know that," Victoria said. "We're not going to just drop the whole thing in your lap and fold our hands. It's up to all of us, of course. We have to think, think, think!"

They thought.

"Maybe," Robert said, "if we really have to chase him off, maybe we could play ghosts. You know, dress up in sheets and sneak into the Hollisters' after dark and haunt him? Hey, come to think of it, there's some old pieces of chain out in the stable! We could rattle them and groan—"

"Oh pooh!"

"No, listen! Remember when Papa read 'Sleepy Hollow' to us? It worked on Ichabod Crane, didn't it—playing ghost?"

"Oh, Bobbie! The whole point was that there was this *legend* about the ghost on the horse, and Ichabod Crane was half expecting to meet him anyway. Mr. Sweeney isn't Ichabod and Hollister's isn't haunted. It's probably the least haunted house in the whole country, Bobbie."

"Well, it was just an idea . . ."

They thought some more.

"Wait a minute," Susan said. "You say he's after your Mama's money. What if he thought your Mama had lost it all?"

"Ah!" said Victoria, widening her eyes. "He'd show a clean pair of heels then! But why should he think that?"

"Well, I just thought we could give him the idea somehow. Send him a letter, or—I don't know."

"That just might do it, though," Victoria mused. "If only you were taller, Bobbie! We could put a pair of false whiskers on you, and you could meet him somewhere and scrape up an acquaintance and say"—she jumped up and assumed an exaggerated masculine swagger—" 'Heard about

Mrs. Walker? Lost all her money, poor woman. Extraordinary case, sir!' "

"That'd be fun," Robert laughed. "But he'd recognize me, Vic, he's not blind."

"I know . . ."

There was another interval of cogitation.

"Wait a minute!" Robert suddenly whispered, "*He wouldn't recognize Susan!*"

"Ah!" said Victoria. They looked at Susan hopefully.

"Don't stare at me like that," Susan said. "I'm trying to think." She was ahead of them in realizing that Mr. Sweeney wouldn't recognize her. And it was no use protesting that it was none of her business. The whole course of recent events had made it her business. She was it, willy-nilly.

Ever since Robert's mention of "Sleepy Hollow" her mind had been turning over memories of all the books she had read. There should be an idea somewhere among them . . . She thought of Mr. Toad, humbugging his way across the country in his washerwoman's disguise. No good in this case . . . Disguises and acting, though —that was right in her line. "Wait a minute, wait a minute," she muttered. "Let's see, there was . . . Tom Sawyer, or—

"Huckleberry Finn!" she cried. "Remember?"

The Walkers both looked blank. "What's that?" Robert asked.

"You know! It's a book—*Huckleberry Finn?* Oh, maybe it hasn't been written yet . . . Anyway, what was it now? They were going down the river on this raft. How did it go? Huck wanted to keep someone away from the raft, they were in a rowboat, I think . . . And he—ah! What would Mr. Sweeney do if your Mama had smallpox?"

"Don't," said Robert in a thin voice.

"No, no! I just mean if he *thought* she had it."

Victoria was staring at her open-mouthed. "Susan Shaw," she whispered, "you positively frighten me."

"Well, it worked in *Huckleberry Finn*. Is smallpox serious or not?"

"*Serious?*" Victoria looked at her brother. "Remember Ginny Schmidt?" Robert nodded solemnly. "She *died* of it."

"All right! Don't look so shocked, it has to be drastic if it's going to work at all. It won't chase him away if I just say your Mama's lost her money—he'll only come over to see if it's true. We've got to *scare* him. Now, if I can just get him by himself for a while—"

"Bobbie," Victoria said decisively, "run and see if he's anywhere in sight. Go on, go on, you can look out Mama's window. Susan, that's the most incredible idea I ever heard in my whole life! You should be a man with a mind like yours!"

"Oh, let me think, will you?" Susan said, chewing her knuckle.

Robert came running back in a minute. "Yes, he's in the Hollisters' back yard right now, smoking a cigar!" Then, in a dubious voice, "Listen, I don't know about this. It's a thumping big lie. I don't know whether—"

"It's a stratagem," Victoria said firmly. "It's a kind of test. What would *you* do if you heard that I'd lost all my money and had smallpox?"

"Don't talk that way, Vic."

"What would you do? Would you run away?"

"No, I'd bring you all my money, if I had any, and I'd nurse you back to health."

"All right! So would any real gentleman. Now, if Mr. Sweeney runs away, he isn't *fit* to marry Mama, is he? And if he stays—oh," she threw her hands in the air, "then I give up, he's a better man than I thought. Anyway, we have to know. For Mama's sake."

"I've got it!" Susan said. "I'm going to be a servant girl. Have you got that kind of a dress, Vicky?"

"Umm . . . I guess you could wear my mourning dress, it's all black. But the material's too good for a—"

"That's all right, it could be a hand-me-down. Now, let's see . . . I'll need a little trunk or a bundle or something. I'm going to pretend I'm running away."

"Wait a minute." Victoria rummaged around in her chest of drawers. "How about this old shawl?"

"Yes, that'll do. We can wrap a pillow up in it. Do servant girls wear hats? Never mind, I'll pretend I came away so fast that I forgot mine. Does Mr. Sweeney know Mr. Branscomb?"

"I don't know. Do you, Bobbie?"

"I don't know—don't think so. Why?"

"The horse and buggy out front," Susan explained. "If your Mama's supposed to be sick the doctor would be here."

"Dr. Balch drives a dogcart," Robert said.

"Well, does he know Dr. Balch?"

"I don't think so," Victoria said.

"Oh, well, the whole thing's a big gamble anyway. We'll just have to hope. Help me off with this dress, Vicky."

"You may leave the room, Robert," Victoria said. "I know, you can scout the territory. See what Maggie's doing. We'll have to smuggle Sue down the back stairs. Oh, this is all so exciting, I can't *stand* it!"

☙ 8 · SUSAN'S GREATEST ROLE ☙

Susan had not noticed Hollister's before; it was on the opposite side of the Walker's house from the garden where she had wandered during the night, and it could not be seen from Victoria's room. It was a little square box of a place, deeply shaded by elms, with a chicken run along the far side.

They crouched by a gap in the hedge, breathing hard and studying the enemy.

"Beast!" Victoria hissed. "Look at him swagger!"

"Here, smudge my face, will you?" Susan whispered. Robert grubbed up a handful of dirt. "Just a smidgen, now, don't overdo it; nothing spoils a performance like a bad make-up job. Wish we'd brought a mirror. How's my hair, Vicky? Muss it up a little, will you? Maybe you can pull some strands out of my braids. I want it kind of bird's-nesty. Do you mind if I make just a little tear in the sleeve?"

"Oh no. I don't know why I kept the dress anyway, it's too small for me now."

"Here, use my pocketknife, Sue."

"Thanks. There, that's it. Now, let's see . . . some wrinkles in my stockings."

"*Do* look the other way, Robert!"

"There! Now please don't giggle or anything, you'll spoil the whole show."

"Oh, I couldn't! I'm just ready to *die*!"

"Me too," said Robert in a shaking voice.

Susan herself was feeling the familiar pangs of stage fright. 'Calm down,' she thought, 'calm down, it won't be any worse than last year when what's-her-name forgot her lines and had hysterics . . .' But she knew it could be much worse. This was not an audience already inclined to be sympathetic that she had to convince, but a man who was persistent and perhaps unscrupulous in getting what he wanted; a man, moreover, who didn't know his lines, but would have to take all his cues from her. 'Just feed him a little information at a time,' she warned herself. 'Build it up, don't blurt it all out at once.' She stood up, remembering all the servant girls she had read of in books or seen in the movies or on the stage. She would have to say "sir" frequently. It might be well to whine a bit . . .

Now or never. She took a deep breath, squeezed through the hedge, and advanced to meet the foe.

Mr. Sweeney was—handsome! She didn't know what she had been expecting, but it certainly wasn't this. She was seized with panic. This distinguished man a scoundrel? Victoria must be mistaken! What was she doing here, what had she gotten herself into? She checked her approach. But no, she must go on—they were watching her; Victoria had said that they *had* to know; if she spoiled it now there might not be another chance.

Her numbed legs would hardly propel her forward again. "Please, sir," she quavered, dropping an awkward little curtsey.

Mr. Sweeney removed his cigar, regarded her for a

moment, then smiled. And with that smile Susan recognized whom she was dealing with. 'Oho, you slick one!' she thought, with a surge of returning confidence. 'I'll bet you've been practising that in front of a mirror! But if you think it's going to make *me* swoon, you're wrong.' Now that she was closer her first impression of him began to change. Handsome, yes. But he held his cigar in a fastidious way, in a hand that was white and soft. His mustache was clipped with mathematical precision. His derby was tilted slightly to reveal a wave of black hair so perfect that it seemed to have been lacquered in place.

"Ah, my dear," he said in a smooth, low voice. "May I be of any assistance?"

"Please, sir, I'm in awful trouble. I just lost my job—my *position*, I mean—through no fault of my own."

"Ah," Mr. Sweeney murmured, "distressing, distressing." His smile lost a little of its brilliance.

"Please, sir, I just wanted to ask you a little favor, you looked like such a kind gentleman."

"Anything in my power, my dear. But may I suggest that you approach me later—say in two weeks' time? I expect to be in circumstances then that will enable me to consider your application. If your references are suitable, of course."

"Oh, thank you, sir. But I didn't mean you should hire me, though I'm sure it'd be a pleasure to work for a kind gentleman like you. I was hoping for a ride to town, if you'll pardon me, sir."

"My dear, it pains me to have to say no. At any other time I would leap to your assistance. But it so happens that I do not intend to return to town for several days. I am here on a matter of some delicacy." He drew on his cigar with a flourish, and fired that dazzling smile at her again. "A matter—I am sure you will understand—of the heart."

'Oh, you ham!' she thought. 'I suppose you expect me to giggle and blush.' Blushing to order was impossible, but she did manage a fair giggle. "Oh, sir, I'm sure the lady will be the luckiest—"

"Therefore," Mr. Sweeney went on, "if you will be so kind, I will resume those tender reveries in which I was engaged when you first found me. Perhaps one of the agricultural gentlemen down the lane will give you a lift."

The scene was threatening to slip out of control. It was time to offer him the bait.

"Oh, sir," she sniffled, "I hate to go on bothering you, sir, but I don't know where to turn. I *am* in trouble, sir. They turned me away *without my wages*." 'Ask me why,' she prayed.

"Really?" Mr. Sweeney murmured. "It grieves me even to entertain the idea, my girl, but perhaps you deserved it." And with that he turned his back on her and began to walk away.

"Oh, sir," she bleated in sincere desperation, "wait!" She trotted after him, trying to think of what to say next. But all that would come to her was "wait."

Mr. Sweeney swung around on her. "Do not presume too far on my patience, miss! I can do nothing for you. No—stay." He plunged a hand into his pocket, felt about carefully, and produced a dime. "If this can alleviate your distress in any measure I shall be gratified. No, no, do not thank me. Good day!"

"Oh, you are a gentleman, sir, *so* kind of you. But begging your pardon, sir, I didn't deserve to be turned away. I always gave satisfactory service—"

"Good day!"

"Satisfactory service," she persisted, raising her voice. "Mrs. Walker always said—"

Aha! That had hit the target. Why hadn't she mentioned the name earlier? 'He's listening now,' she thought; 'throw out that lead about your wages again.'

"Did I understand you to say Mrs. Walker?"

"Yes, sir. I just came from her house. She was very sorry to turn me away without my—"

But Mr. Sweeney still wouldn't take his cue. "It may interest you to know, my dear," he said in his smoothest voice, "that my connection with the Walkers is on a familiar, not to say intimate, footing."

"Yes, sir," she said warily. What was he driving at?

"Therefore," he purred, "I find myself somewhat at a loss to explain why I never saw you in that household."

She fought down a surge of panic. "I-I'm sure you wouldn't have noticed me, sir," she gulped. "I was—in the—in the kitchen. All the time. Maggie was training me out there." A faint hope occurred to her, and she clutched at it. "Oh!" she exclaimed, trying to make it sound like a cry of pleased recognition. "Why, you must be Mr. Sweeney that they all speak so well of!"

It worked. Mr. Sweeney displayed his smile and gave a little flourish with his cigar. Then his eyes narrowed, and in a silky bantering tone he said:

"So—satisfied with your work, were they?"

"Oh, yes, sir. They—"

"And yet you were discharged from service?"

"Yes, sir. You see—"

"Without your wages, if I understand correctly."

"Yes, sir. Mrs. Walk—"

"Perhaps," Mr. Sweeney said, still smiling, but with a cruel little quirk at the corners of his mouth, "perhaps there was a little matter of spoons disappearing, or something like that, eh?"

"Oh, *no*, sir!"

"Would you still accept a ride from me if I told you that we should go directly to a police station?"

"Certainly, sir. I have nothing to—"

"Oh, well," he said, tiring of his game and turning away. "It's no concern of mine what you've been up to. I have no doubt Mrs. Walker was fully justified, however. Good day."

And here, suddenly, was the chance she'd been waiting for.

"Oh, sir, I wouldn't say a word against Mrs. Walker. I'm sure she would have paid my wages. *If she'd been able to.*"

Mr. Sweeney's cigar was arrested halfway to his mouth. "I do not quite apprehend your meaning, my dear," he said carefully.

"Oh," she gasped, putting her hand to her face. "I shouldn't have mentioned it, I'm sure."

"Did I understand you to mean can't? Or won't?"

"Can't, sir. Oh, but I shouldn't have said it. I'm sure they don't want their troubles talked about."

"See here, my girl, I think you had better explain yourself."

Susan retreated a step, averting her eyes so that he wouldn't see the triumph that was shining in them. It was just like playing the old childhood game of I Have A Secret I Won't Tell. She could tell by the sudden wary tone in his voice that he was hooked.

He was also impatient. Seizing her by the arm, he said, "Now, just what do you mean, trouble?"

"Money trouble, sir," she stammered.

His grip tightened. "All right, out with it. I've got to know—as a friend of the family."

She almost reeled under a burst of inspiration. "Well, perhaps if you were to make it worth my while, sir," she whined.

For a moment it looked as if she had gone too far. Then Mr. Sweeney smiled—a genuine, appreciative smile. "Aha! Artful little sharper, aren't you? I think we understand each other, my dear." He explored his pocket again, pulled out a half-dollar, and held it up just beyond reach. "Now—short and sweet!"

"Well, sir," she said in a low voice, keeping her eyes on the coin, "a few days ago Mrs. Walker got a letter. I heard her and Miss Victoria talking about it. Really by accident, sir, I'm not an eavesdropper."

"Never mind that."

"They were crying as if their hearts would break, sir, and Mrs. Walker's been shut up in her room for two days and won't eat anything, and she's crying something awful. So I asked Maggie what it was, and she had hysterics—"

"I said never mind that. *Out* with it!"

"It was a confidence man," she whispered. "He had an invention or a—a gold mine or something, and he talked Mrs. Walker into putting her money in it. And now they've found out he's run away to the—to the Continent."

Mr. Sweeney's voice was thick. "What was the take?" he demanded.

"Beg pardon, sir?"

"The *take!*" he snarled, shaking her. "What was in it? How much did he get away with?"

"*Everything!*" she whispered, looking him full in the face for an instant. Then she turned on the tears. "Oh, sir, they only owe me for a month, and they can't even pay that!"

Mr. Sweeney's face swelled and darkened. The half-dollar dropped from his hand. He whipped his derby off, smashed it with his fist, and ground out a noise, half hiss and half strangled shout, between his clenched teeth.

"Oh, sir!" she cried. "Do me one more kindness, *please.* Take me away from here—"

"Now you cut along!" he grated. "I've heard all I want. Get out." He hurled his cigar to the ground and stamped on it.

"Save me, save me!" she wept, flinging herself against him. "Oh, I'm so scared! I must get away, please help me!"

"Here, what's the hurry? What are you hiding from me?"

"Oh, I'm so scared! Mrs. Walker—oh, it's too horrible!"

"What? What? She kill herself?"

"No, sir, but she's so sick."

"Huh! Don't wonder. Sick myself."

"No, *really* sick! Take me away, I don't want to die!"

"Wait a minute!" said Mr. Sweeney hoarsely. "What's she got?"

"The—doctor says—if she's lucky enough to live—she'll be scarred—for l-l-life!"

"Great Scott!" Mr. Sweeney choked, hastily backing away. "Smallpox!"

"Take me away!" Susan sobbed, clinging to him. "I was just talking to Miss Victoria, and she—she—she said she felt all over queer herself!"

"*Get away from me!*" Mr. Sweeney shouted. He pushed her violently, lost his balance, and sat down. "Get away! Get away! Touching me! Breathing on me! You little—" His fingers closed around a fragment of brick in the grass. He scrambled to his feet and raised his weapon. "Get away from me!" he panted.

They both turned and fled at the same instant—Mr. Sweeney toward the house, Susan toward the hedge. She stumbled, for she had actually succeeded in frightening herself, and was still wildly weeping; but in her mind sang the triumphant thought, 'Oh, if only Elsie Mautner could have seen that! She'd never dare walk on a stage again!'

9 · MRS. WALKER'S CONFESSION

The violence of Mr. Sweeney's reaction had, in fact, frightened all of them; even Susan had not expected to be *that* successful. A fit of hysterical giggling overcame them as they made their way back to the house, and continued for some time after they had regained Victoria's room.

"My!" Victoria said when they had calmed down somewhat. "That was simply *inspired*."

"Well, I've had some experience in dramatics," Susan said modestly. "You were right, Vicky, you were absolutely right about him. I told him that a confidence man had run away with all your Mama's money, and you should have seen his face!"

"Was that when he smashed his hat?"

"Yes! Oh, he was so mad I thought he'd have ap-ap—what-d'you-call-it."

"Apoppalepsy," said Robert.

"Oh, the brute!" Victoria said, shaking her fist. "I wish he had. Foiled in his villainous plans! I wish you were big enough to thrash him, Bobbie.—What are you looking so solemn about?"

"Well, the thing is," Robert said, "we don't know whether it's really worked."

"Of course it's worked! What are you talking about? Didn't you see him run?"

"Certainly I saw him run, but that's *now*. How about later when he starts to think it over? What if he begins to check up? He could ask at the bank about Mama's money, and then he'd find out it was all a big fib."

"Stratagem," Victoria insisted.

"All right, stratagem. But he'll call it lying, and then we'll be in trouble."

"No you won't," Susan said. "*I* did it, not you. He didn't even see you."

"No, but he'll probably suspect we were accomplices if he finds out it wasn't true."

"Well, I don't care," Victoria said. "We've unmasked him now and we know he's a villain. That's all that matters. He can even come back if he wants to—once Mama is warned it won't do him a bit of good."

"All right, but *how* are we going to warn Mama?"

"Oh, don't be so slow!" she cried in exasperation. "We'll tell her that he's just after her money."

"You're the one that's being slow, Vic. The first thing Mama will ask is, *how do we know*."

"Oh my goodness!" Victoria said in a small voice. "That's right . . ."

"The thing is, we really did lie to him. I don't care what you call it, Vic, we did. And if Mama finds out— well, you know what she'll think about that. It won't make any difference to her *why* we did it."

"Now wait a minute," Susan said. "Let's not get panicky. If it works the whole question will never even come up."

"If . . ." Victoria said gloomily.

They stared at each other in silence.

"What's that?" Victoria suddenly whispered.

"Horse!" Robert said.

They rushed to the window, but it was only Mr. Branscomb driving away.

"Maybe," Susan said hopefully, "maybe Mr. Sweeney left while we were coming up the back stairs. We couldn't have heard him from there, could we?"

"Maybe he hasn't left at all," Robert said.

"Let's look out Mama's window and see," Victoria suggested.

"That won't do any good. You can't see Hollister's stable from there."

"Let's look anyway—I can't *stand* it any more. Maybe we can see something—"

"Ssh! Someone's coming!" Susan whispered.

There was a knock at the door, and Mrs. Walker's voice said, "Bobbie? Vicky?"

"Under the bed!" Robert mouthed silently. Susan flung herself to the floor and wriggled out of sight.

"Children, children!" said Mrs. Walker, opening the door. "Such a thumping and bumping! You haven't been quarreling, I hope?"

"Oh, no, Mama!" Victoria said in a strained voice. "We were just . . ."

"Just talking," Robert croaked.

"Well! I hope the time will soon come when you won't find it necessary to stamp your feet while you talk. What is the matter, anyway? You both look as if I'd caught you with your hands in the cookie jar."

"You-you-you just surprised us, Mama," Robert said faintly. "Here, won't you have a chair?"

"Thank you, Bobbie. They've been teaching you well at school, I see." The chair creaked. "I think you had better sit down, too. You too, Vicky. We have something to discuss."

There was a thick silence.

"Well, children," Mrs. Walker said at last. "I think it's time we had a very serious talk about Mr. Sweeney."

She could not have startled them more if she had fired a gun. Even Susan jumped a little under the four-poster, and felt her face go hot.

"Oh, come, children, there's no need to blush! I think it's no secret, is it, that Mr. Sweeney has been—well, interested in us for quite a while?"

Silence from Robert and Victoria. Perhaps they were shaking their heads.

"In fact," Mrs. Walker went on, "it's no secret that he's proposed to me on numerous occasions. Until now I've thought it best to refuse him. That's no secret, either. But . . ."

"But wh-wh-what, Mama?" Victoria husked.

"Well . . . he's made a very handsome offer, my dears!"

"You mean you've seen him already?" Victoria blurted out.

"What do you mean, 'already?' Is he here?"

"He's at the Hollisters'," Robert said miserably. "I think."

"Oh. Well, he said he'd be here soon, without mentioning exactly when. No, I haven't seen him since last time; but I had a letter from him yesterday."

"Oh," said Victoria. "Well, what is his handsome offer?" Susan could imagine how Victoria's mouth twisted on the word "handsome."

"Why, he speaks of a military school for you, Bobbie! Isn't that splendid? Just what you've been wanting. And a very well-known finishing school for *you*, dear. I'm very pleased to find that he has your welfare so much at heart."

"What about *your* welfare?" Victoria bristled.

"Oh, I don't count," Mrs. Walker laughed. "I'm just an old woman, Vicky. I've had my life—yours is still ahead of you, and it's yours that I'm thinking of."

"You're *not* an old woman, and you *do* count. Mr. Sweeney—goodness!" Victoria suddenly gasped, "you're not in *love* with him, are you, Mama?"

"Well," said Mrs. Walker evasively, "love seems very important when you're young. But you'll find as you grow older that duty comes first."

"Duty to *him?*"

"No, my dear, duty to you and Bobbie. It's simply not right for two growing children to be without a Papa. I've been very concerned about it for some time, and now that—now that things have reached a certain stage . . . Well, what I'm trying to say is that I must seriously begin to consider your future."

"Oh, Mama!" Victoria wailed. "I don't blame you for worrying about us, but you could do so much better than Mr. Sweeney! If only you'd go to town a little more often."

"Victoria, are you proposing that I go out and throw myself at men's heads?"

"Of course not, Mama! If you'd just visit friends and—well, there'd be dinners and parties—and you'd—you couldn't help being introduced to—"

"I'm afraid I've lost all my heart for society since your Papa died . . . And, you see, Mr. Sweeney has been kind enough to come to me, instead of the other way around . . . I know you're not very favorably impressed by him, Vicky—"

"I think he's horrid!" Victoria whispered.

"Oh . . . What do you think, Bobbie?"

Robert made some inarticulate, but negative, noises.

Mrs. Walker sighed. "I suppose he is a little—too polished, perhaps . . ." Suddenly her voice broke. "Oh, children, I'm so tired, so tired! I can't think any more, I don't know what to—" Then she regained control of herself, and continued, almost harshly, with: "Well, no matter. There's nothing more to discuss. My own feelings do not concern anyone but myself, and my duty toward you two is clear. Your duty toward me, as children toward their mother, is to yield to my decision. I shall—I shall accept Mr. Sweeney's offer."

"Mama—"

"Please, Vicky! There is nothing more to discuss."

Victoria's voice trembled with a desperate resolve. "I just wanted to ask a question, Mama. How much money does Mr. Sweeney have?"

"Victoria! I'm shocked at you! That's the sort of thing a lady *never* asks a gentleman!"

"I'm sorry, Mama. But that's the sort of thing a *gentleman* would make clear, isn't it? And he hasn't said anything about it, has he?"

"Mr. Sweeney is always very well turned out, as you know. And I'm sure he wouldn't be speaking of expensive schools for you two if he weren't prepared—"

"—prepared to spend *your* money," Victoria broke in. "That's all he's after, Mama. He doesn't care a fig for *us*. He's a fortune-hunter and a scoundrel, and I'd say the same to his face!"

"Victoria Albertine, that is a very serious accusation. You had better take it back and apologize for it, or explain yourself."

'Oh oh!' Susan thought, clenching her hands until they ached. 'Now it comes out . . .' She knew that Victoria would not back down, but would confess what they had done rather than see her mother make the fatal mistake; and she realized that at that point she herself would be honor-bound to come out from under the bed and take the blame. The ensuing complications would not bear thinking about.

"Well, it's true, Mama," Victoria began bravely. "You see, about an hour ago we—"

There was a knock at the door.

"Come in! Yes, Maggie?"

"Note for you, Mum," said a hoarse voice.

"Thank you, Maggie. Does it require an answer?"

"No'm. Mrs. Hollister brought it. Queerest thing! Herself's not the kind to be passing notes. She always spoke right out before."

"Thank you, Maggie."

The door closed. There was an unbearable silence.

"Well," Mrs. Walker said at last.

"What is it, Mama?" Robert croaked.

Mrs. Walker's voice was flat. "It seems, my dears, that we have been worrying ourselves to no purpose. Mr. Sweeney has changed his mind."

"Mama, what does he say?"

"He says that he has received certain information that makes it necessary for him to withdraw his offer."

So—their scheme had worked. But Susan felt no triumph in the thought. Confession was inevitable now; and that being the case, she might as well come forth at once and tell Mrs. Walker that she was the one who had supplied Mr. Sweeney with his "certain information." She was just about to roll out from under the four-poster when Mrs. Walker stopped her dead by saying quietly:

"I owe you an apology, Vicky. It seems you were right."

"I-I-I—" Victoria stammered, evidently as astonished as Susan was by this unexpected turn.

"Apparently he *is* a fortune-hunter," Mrs. Walker went on. "I don't know how he got his certain information so quickly; but then they do say that bad news travels fast . . ."

"What bad news?" Robert whispered. "Why are you crying, Mama?"

"I hoped I wouldn't have to tell you, children. I was praying that Mr. Branscomb could set things right—it's been coming a long time, I'm afraid—we've done everything we could—dear Mr. Branscomb has been moving heaven and earth to help us—oh!" she sobbed, "Mr. Sweeney was my last hope for your future! We're ruined, children—we haven't a penny left in the world!"

⚔ 10 · QUEST FOR A MAP ⚔

Susan could not see what effect this announcement had on Robert and Victoria, but she could imagine it from the state of her own feelings. She could not have been more shocked if her own father had announced his ruin.

Robert, as befitted a soldier and the man of the family, was the first to recover. "Don't worry, Mama," he quavered. "I'll go to work. I can be an office boy, or work for a newspaper, or something . . ."

"That's my brave Bobbie."

There was a confused moment of sobbing and murmuring and back-patting, which, as it turned out, was fortunate; because at that very moment Susan said "Oh!" rather loudly, without being able to help herself, and she would have been heard if the Walkers had not been so occupied. It was Robert's mention of the word "newspaper" that did it. Newspaper! She had been looking at one just before getting on the elevator . . .

When Mrs. Walker had regained some measure of control over her voice, she said, "It's far from hopeless, children. We'll—we'll sell the house. Mr. Branscomb says it will be hard to find a buyer, it's so far from town, but we'll be able to borrow something on it meanwhile. I'm going to write to Cousin Jane; she'll be willing to take us in for a while, and then we can—we can look about us and see what's to be done. Vicky, dear, you're so pale! I'm sorry I frightened you, but the thing has to be faced. We'll just have to be brave, that's all. The Walkers may be down but they've never been out!"

"I'm not out," said Robert.

"You're being wonderful, dear. But then I knew you would be. Well! Come along, we'll all have some hot tea. Remember what your Papa always said: 'Never make an important decision without drinking a cup of tea and having a good night's sleep.' We'll just pretend that he's still with us, and behave as he'd expect us to; and everything will turn out all right, I'm sure."

"We'll be down in a minute, Mama. I want to talk to Vic—privately, please."

"All right, dear. Come as soon as you can. I'll have Maggie put the kettle on."

The door had no sooner closed than Susan was scrambling out from under the bed. "Listen!" she hissed excitedly. "Listen, I—"

"Gosh, Sue, did you hear that?" Robert said. "We've lost all our money—really lost it!"

"Listen, don't worry! I know where—"

"It's a judgment on us!" Victoria whispered. Her face was very pinched and white. "We told a big lie, and it's coming true, to punish us. Oh!" she cried, throwing herself across the bed and bursting into tears, "why didn't I listen to you, Bobbie? You said it was wrong. Now it's coming true, it's coming true! Oh, if Mama gets smallpox now, I'll just kill myself!"

"Don't talk that way, Vic. It couldn't be our doing. Mama said it's been coming for a long time."

"Oh, listen, both of you!" Susan cried, dancing up and

down. "*Listen.* You don't have to worry about a thing! I *know where a treasure is buried!*"

"What?" said Robert, turning to her with a stupefied air.

"Treasure! Thousands and thousands of dollars, just up the street from here!"

"But how do you—how do you—?"

"Oh! Whew, let me catch my breath!" She sat down on the bed beside Victoria, who was gaping at her incredulously. "I read about it in the paper, it was all over the front page—"

"But if it was in the paper that means it's been found already," Robert said. "Anyway, I didn't read anything about—"

"No! Will you please just listen? It was in a 1960 paper. I read about it just before I came here. It hasn't been found, it won't be found for years and years! It's there right now, waiting for us to find it first. The paper even had a map showing where it is!"

"Great Caesar! How much did you say it was?"

"Oh, I forget exactly, but it was thousands. Enough to save you and your Mama, anyway. We're going to find it—I'm going right down the elevator as soon as I can and bring back the map. So don't let your Mama do anything yet. Don't let her sell the house or write to Cousin Jane—"

"Children?" came faintly from below.

"Coming, Mama!" Robert shouted. "What are we going to tell her, Sue?"

"I don't know, you'll have to think of something. Just try to get her to put everything off until we can find the treasure."

"Susan Shaw," Victoria whispered, "I think you came from heaven!"

"Oh, don't be mushy, for goodness sake! Go on, go on. I have to think."

As soon as she was alone she kicked off her shoes and

padded silently up and down the room, chewing her knuckle. It was all very well to put up a confident front for Robert and Victoria, but now that they were gone doubts began to creep in. She could get the map, all right—but would it be of any use? There was a vast difference between the city streets of 1960 and the open country of 1881. The whole thing depended on where the Walker's house stood—that was the only point of reference they had to start from. *Was the house standing on the same spot that the apartment building would some day occupy?*

'Well, it just has to be,' she thought. 'The elevator didn't go sideways or back and forth—it *felt* as if it went straight up, anyway. Ward Lane out there does look a little farther off than it should be, but then they could have widened it toward the house when they made Ward Street out of it. It just *has* to be in the same place, that's all . . .'

Early in the evening Robert returned to the room. With an expression of studious innocence he came up to the bedside stand, and proceeded to unload from his pockets a large quantity of bread-and-butter sandwiches, cold lamb chops, cold boiled potatoes, cookies, and nuts.

"I usually can't do this well," he said modestly, "but Mama and Vic couldn't eat much at supper. I can *always* eat. I guess if tomorrow were Judgment Day I could still eat. As a matter of fact . . ." he added delicately, staring at a cookie.

"Help yourself," Susan said. "I couldn't possibly eat all this. Thanks for bringing it up."

"Welcome . . . Sue?"

"Mm?"

"Do you really think it'll work?"

"Sure it will," she said, with more conviction than she felt. "Why not?"

"Well . . . there's something wrong somewhere. I can't put my finger on it, but it bothers me."

"Look. The money was buried sometime around the Civil War. Nobody's dug it up yet. So it's still there. What's wrong about that? All we have to do is find the place."

"Well . . . When are you going down in the elevator?"

"Soon as it's dark."

"That's an odd thing. I should think you'd go *up* in the elevator. You know, you sort of think of old time on the bottom and new time piled on top, like a—like a—" He waved his cookie helplessly, swallowed it, and selected another. "I don't know. It's awfully queer any way you think of it. Can I watch?"

"Of . . . course," she said, yawning until her ears cracked. The late conversation of last night, this afternoon's performance for Mr. Sweeney, the strain of worrying about finding the treasure, and now all this food . . . She crawled into the four-poster, numb with fatigue.

"Wake me up when it's dark?" she mumbled.

"Sure, Sue. Don't you want this chop?"

"Mm-mm . . ."

Robert happily fell to. Susan slept.

"Sue. Sue. Susan!"

"Urrmmf?" she said. Victoria was an indistinct shape bending over her in the dark. "Time is it?"

"Shh! It's after twelve, I think. I was going to wake you much earlier, but I didn't dare till Mama fell asleep, and then I dropped off myself. Here, while you're waking up I'll go get Bobbie, he'll be furious if he misses it."

Susan stretched and scrubbed her face until she was awake. Victoria returned with Robert, who glimmered ghost-like in his nightshirt.

"We have to be extra quiet," he whispered. "Mama's still tossing around. Hey, Vic, don't light the candle yet."

"Please don't say 'hey,' Bobbie," Victoria sighed.

Robert, as foraging expert, took the lead. They crept down the back stairs, paused to light their candle in the kitchen, and proceeded more quickly to the hallway. The clock said twenty to one.

"It was right here," said Susan, pointing to the wainscotting. "But I don't know where the button is. Do you see one?"

"Button?" Robert said. "What's the button for?"

"You push it and the elevator comes up."

"Oh. Is it like a shirt button or a shoe button?"

"Neither—it's a black knob. Help me find it, will you?"

They searched the paneling inch by inch, holding the candle close, but could find nothing.

"What if I *can't* go back?" Susan said in a small voice.

"Nonsense!" said Victoria. "The old woman gave you three trips, didn't she? Try pushing the place where the button *should* be."

"Well, that might do it. About here, I guess." She pressed her thumb against the wood. "Doesn't feel like—" she muttered. "Wait a minute." She put her ear against the wainscotting. Ah! Faintly, as if from the depths of a canyon, came the sound of mechanisms stirring to life.

"It's all right!" she said. "Whew! It may take a while, though, it's the slowest old elevator in the world."

"Shall we wait here for you, Sue?"

"Well, I don't know. I'll have to explain to Daddy, that'll take some time; and then I'll have to persuade him to let me come up again, that'll take a while—"

"Hey!" Robert said faintly. "It's making a noise!"

"Of course it's making a noise, it always does. Here it comes."

"Sighhh!" said the wainscotting. "Rummmble." It split into two sections that folded back to the right.

"Great Caesar!" The candle in Robert's hand made a wild dip as he clutched his sister's arm. "It's—it's deep in there," he whispered.

"Same old elevator," said Susan, getting into it. "Now listen, I'll come back as soon as I can. You don't have to wait if you don't want to, I can find my way up to Vicky's room by now. Dont worry about me, it's perfectly safe. Bye."

She pressed the third-floor button. The wainscotting sighed and began to close.

A scrabbling noise suddenly made itself heard in the shadows of the hallway. "Oooh!" Victoria squeaked, jumping into the air as something black hurtled past her legs and into the elevator.

"Stop that!" Susan cried. "Get out of here!" But it was too late—the door closed, the elevator began to groan its way downward.

"Here, you—*stop* that—oh, poor mousie! Drop it! *Drop* it!" She slapped with all her strength.

"Mrrowr!" said Toby, flattening his ears. The mouse shot from his jaws and took refuge in a corner.

"Come *here*, you nasty old cat, let it alone! Now I'll have to take you back—no, I can't, it'll waste a trip. Here, behave yourself! Ouch!"

Toby had suddenly discovered that his world was not only too small, but disconcertingly in motion. "Wow!" he said, using his claws.

"Stop it!" she panted. "You're tearing my dress! Oh, I still have Victoria's clothes on! What if anybody sees me?" I'll just have to pretend not to see them—hold still! No, I'll pretend I'm rehearsing a part in a play. *Ouch*, you—"

She and Toby battled all the way to the third floor, both of them becoming considerably disheveled in the process. Toby could draw blood, but Susan had size and strength on her side, and was determined to save the mouse from destruction. By the time the door opened again she had managed to get an arm-lock on the cat and one hand clamped around his chops.

How strange the hallway looked, with its rows of doors and the dim night lights! And how strange it smelled—as if the air, tinctured with cigarette smoke and Mr. Bodoni's carpet shampoo, had not been in circulation for a long time. She had only been away since Wednesday, and yet it felt like years. 'Well, it has been years, in a way,' she thought; 'almost a century!' What was that odd voice vibrating in the stillness? It was tiny and metallic, wailing behind one of the closed doors:

> Yew broke mah hear-r-r-rt
> When yew went uh-way-y-y . . .

A television set! But of course there were television sets—she was in the twentieth century again.

Toby had calmed down now that his horizon had expanded and the floor was steady again. She kept her grip on him, however, just in case, and peered out cautiously. No one in the hallway! Swiftly she tiptoed to her apartment door and opened it—

'Oh oh!'

The table lamp was lit. There was a policeman sitting in the armchair. His blouse was loosened, his chin rested on his chest, and he wheezed faintly in his sleep. Mrs. Clutchett, mummied in blankets, snored on the sofa.

'What . . . ?' she thought, closing the door again with exquisite care. 'What's going on here? A policeman in the apartment? Has there been a burglary? But why should Mrs. Clutchett—?· Oh! It must be me! They probably think I've been kidnapped! Or that I ran away! Oh, poor Daddy. I'll have to tell him at once—

'But I can't,' she thought, arresting her hand on the knob. 'Maybe I could explain to Daddy, but the policeman will never believe me. And if they think I ran away once they won't let me go again—and if I don't get back soon Mrs. Walker will start selling the house and writing to Cousin Jane, and Bobbie and Vicky'll think that I've deserted them just when they need me most . . . What to do, what to do?'

"Yew broke mah hear-r-r-rt," whined the television set.

'Oh, be quiet!' she thought. 'What a mess . . . Why didn't I think that they might—? I know, I'll write a note. Daddy'll recognize my writing, he won't have to worry any more. Let's see—paper, pencil . . . Basement, that's it. I can get the map there, too.'

She and Toby had another fight on the way down. The clawing and squirming put her in a rage; and when they reached the basement she hurled the cat out the door without even bothering to see if the coast was clear.

Mr. Bodoni made a little extra money by collecting old newspapers from the tenants and selling them, when he had gathered a large pile, to an acquaintance of his in the junk business. Susan hurried to the pile, and searched through the top paper until she found a fashion advertisement with enough blank space to write a note on. There was a stump of pencil in the drawer of Mr. Bodoni's workbench.

'Mmm,' she thought, chewing on it. ' "Dear Daddy, please don't worry about me. I'm *all* right." Now, let's see—the policeman. "Tell the policeman he can go away," that's so he'll know I'm not kidnapped.' She thought for a moment, and added "I'm all right." 'I'll say it twice in a row, just to make sure . . . Better tell him what I'm going to do, so he won't—' And she wrote rapidly, "I have to go back for a little while but please don't worry, it's *perfectly safe*. I'll be home as soon as I can. Love, Susie." 'No use saying *where* I have to go back, he won't believe it anyway.'

"Yow," said Toby, nervously sniffing at a valve on the oil furnace.

"Oh, stop that! You make me sick. Now, where's the paper with the—?" She began to dig down through the stack. "Gosh, what if he hasn't collected the new ones yet—ah!"

FORTUNE FOUND AT CONSTRUCTION SITE

She tore the front page off, folded it small, and thrust it in her pocket. All set!

The elevator door sighed, and trundled shut.

'Oh oh!' she thought. '*Why* can't people go to bed early? Now I'll have to wait until—'

She ran over to the elevator door to see what the arrow was doing. It crept to 1 and stopped. Then it began moving to the left, back to B.

'Oh, someone's coming down!' Aloud she called, "Toby! Come here! Puss Puss?"

Toby was vanishing under the oil tank. She got there just in time to seize the tip of his tail. His muscular protest quivered through her hand like an electric current.

"Oh, come *on*!" she sobbed. Dragging him backwards, his claws scraping across the concrete, she rushed for shelter behind the washing machines. There she crouched in a puddle, holding the cat between her knees and stomach and squeezing his jaws shut with both hands.

It was Mr. Bodoni who emerged from the elevator. He was holding something cradled in his palm, and staring at it with infinite bewilderment.

A long silence.

"Mice," said Mr. Bodoni sorrowfully through his cigar.

A long silence.

"Mice," he repeated. "After all I done."

A long silence.

'Oh, get a *move* on, will you?' Susan raged to herself. Toby's hind claws were sinking into her thigh.

"Traps," said Mr. Bodoni at last, with an air of decision.

He carefully put the dead mouse in his vest pocket, ambled over to his workbench, and began to search for mousetraps in the drawer. There were many to be found, and he had to inspect each one with minute care before putting it in his pocket.

At last he was finished. Now he was going. No, he wasn't. He stopped, turned around, came back to the workbench; brought the stumpy pencil out of the drawer; reached over to the calendar on the wall above the bench; and, muttering each letter aloud, laboriously wrote "Mise" under the date.

Halfway to the elevator he stopped again, and stood a long while vaguely patting his pockets.

"Cheese," said Mr. Bodoni.

He entered the elevator, and was gone.

"Woo-oof!" said Susan, shaking the cramp out of her legs. "I never saw anybody slower in my whole life. Ow, let go of my dress! Honestly, Toby, if you weren't the Walkers' cat I'd just leave you here . . . Well, he has to go out to get the cheese, so we won't have to worry about him any more . . . There, the elevator's free. Now, if you give me any more trouble I'll strangle you."

He did. They grappled all the way to the third floor; and when the elevator door opened, he raked her forearm with his claws, twisted away from her agonized clutch, and bounded into the hallway.

"Toby!" she whispered.

"Hurry!" the television set was shouting tinnily. "This offer will positively not be repeated! This is your last chance! Hurry!"

"Yow!" said Toby, sniffing the carpet. "Wow? *Wowww!*"

There was a muffled snort behind the door of the Shaw's apartment, and the scrape of a chair being thrust back.

'Good grief!' she thought. 'I can't—' She hurled the note into the hallway, and leaned her whole weight against the seventh-floor button. 'Move!' she prayed. 'Move!'

The elevator door closed just in time.

❦ 11 · SUSAN DESPAIRS ❦

Robert and Victoria were still waiting for her, sitting on the floor with the candle between them. They looked worried about something.

"Got it!" Susan whispered triumphantly. She pressed the seventh-floor button to send the elevator back, and got out. "I almost didn't, though. There was a policeman in the apartment and Mr. Bodoni almost found me in the cellar. And oh, I am sorry, but Toby got away from me, and I had to leave him behind or get caught."

"Poor old Toby in the twentieth century!" said Victoria. "Could he tell it was different? How did he like it?"

"He didn't. Look, he ruined your dress with his claws. Don't worry about him, though, Mrs. Clutchett likes cats, she'll take care of him. I'll bring him back the next time. What are you looking so down in the mouth about?"

"Well," said Robert, "I told you I thought something was wrong, only I couldn't put my finger on it—remember? It finally came to me while you were gone. I—I don't think we're going to find that money."

"Why not? Look, here's the map!"

"Oh, I guess the map's all right, but—Well, look. They found it in 1960—I mean they will find it. That means that we can't find it. See?"

"What do you mean, we can't find it? We'll get there years before they do."

"No, look," he said patiently, drawing circles on the floor with his finger. "It's really very simple—if we find it they can't. Because if we find it, *it won't be there in 1960.* Only it is—was—will be. So that means . . ."

"Ohhhh . . ." All the air seemed to go out of Susan with a rush. "Oh, good night!" She dropped to her knees beside them. "I never thought about that."

"So I guess it's all off," said Robert. "It was a good idea, Sue, but—"

They were silent for a while. The clock discreetly said "Whirrr," and chimed the quarter.

"So we'll all end up in the poorhouse," Victoria murmured, rocking herself back and forth. "Cousin Jane isn't rich, she can't keep us forever . . ."

"Don't talk like that," said Robert. "I told you I'm going to get work."

"Well, so am I—I can sew or something. But my goodness, an office boy! A 'prentice seamstress! We won't be able to make anything—"

"Don't forget the house. It's a good house, it'll bring in something."

"I can't *stand* the idea of anybody else living in this house," Victoria wept. "Nobody could love it the way I do. They'll probably put up horrid new wallpaper, and tear out walls, and—"

"Now listen!" Susan said, thumping her fist on the floor. "This is ridiculous! We know exactly where that treasure is—well, almost exactly. We've got a map! There's absolutely nothing to stop us from finding it. Now, here's what I bet happened—will happen. We'll find it, only there'll be an enormous big lot of it, so we'll just take what we need and *we'll leave the rest to be found in 1960!*"

"Ahh!" said the Walkers in one hopeful breath.

"So I'm going to look for it. And I'll go on looking for it until I find it, even if it takes me *months*. So do I have to do it alone, or are you going to help me?"

"Great Caesar! *Are* we! That must be it—we'll leave some! Let's start right now!"

"Not in the dark. First thing tomorrow, though!"

"First thing! Hey, I'm hungry. Let's make a foraging raid!"

"Oh, Robert, please don't say 'hey.' "

"You hungry, Sue?"

"Ravenous!"

"Come on!"

"What will Maggie say?" Victoria sighed.

It rained next morning.

Susan sat by the window chewing her knuckles with frustration, while Robert and Victoria distractedly popped in and out of the room with the latest reports from below. Mrs. Walker, it seemed, was determined to proceed with her plans, and they were powerless to dissuade her.

First it would be Victoria, wringing her hands: "I can't do anything with her, Sue. She's writing to house agents! But what can I do? I can't say anything definite until we actually find the treasure. Oh, this rain!"

And then Robert, who could make biting into a slice of bread-and-butter look like an act of desperation: "Mama's still at it! She says she's had her cup of tea and her night's sleep, and it's no use putting it off any longer. This rain could go on for a week!"

And then Victoria again, thrusting a tragic face around the door to announce, *"She's writing Cousin Jane."*

By ten o'clock Robert had worked himself up to such a pitch that he proposed intercepting Mrs. Walker's letters.

"We couldn't!" Victoria gasped. "Why, that's a crime! It's interfering with government business!"

"Well, we wouldn't destroy them," Robert argued. "Besides, it isn't government business until the mailman has them—is it? What we do is, we take them out of the mailbox and keep them until we find the treasure, and then Mama won't have to send them anyway. Or if we don't find the treasure, we'll post them again, and no harm done."

"We'll find it," said Susan. "Look! Isn't that the sun?"

It was. Their spirits immediately soared.

"Wait here a minute," said Robert. "Have to make arrangements."

In ten minutes he was back. "All right! I told Mama we could face our troubles better if we communed with Nature, and Maggie's making us a picnic lunch. Don't worry, Sue, there'll be enough for you too." He patted his pockets. "I'm bringing a little extra, just in case."

Half an hour later they were in the stable at the back of the property. Susan was delighted with its cool shadowy dimness and the sharp compound of straw, manure, leather, and old wood smells it contained. Swallows were nesting in the rafters; iridescent blue and russet-breasted, they flickered in and out the doorway, calling to each other with a rolling squeak. Twice they came so close that Susan felt the wind of their wings on her face.

Robert was busily rummaging about. "Rope—won't need that, probably. Spade. How many spades, Sue?"

"What?" she said, tearing her attention away from the swallows. "Oh. Just one. What we should have is pointed sticks—you know, to feel down through the dirt with. It's easier than digging."

"Hey! That's a good idea. Never thought of that. Stick. Stick . . ."

"Oh, my goodness!" Victoria gasped, putting her hands to her face. "I just thought. If the treasure's on somebody's property it'll belong to *them*!"

"Oh oh," Robert said.

"Well, let's look at the map," Susan said. She took the newspaper page out of her pocket and unfolded it. "Which way is north, Bobbie?"

"That way."

"All right." She oriented the map, and they all crouched over it. "Yes, that must be right—see, Ward Street goes the same way as Ward Lane. I'm counting on your house being in the same place as the apartment building. The apartment is here—so, one, two, three blocks up Ward, then around the corner and down 93rd. Right here. Where would that be?"

"Knutsen's pasture!" Victoria said in a stricken voice. "It has to be if your blocks are as long as ours. That's Mr. Knutsen's land, so it's his treas—"

"Now that's just where you're wrong!" Robert said triumphantly. "That's county land—Mr. Hollister told me. Somebody had it and lost his money before he could farm it, and now the county holds it for delinquent taxes, and all Mr. Knutsen does is pay them something to run his cows on it!"

"Oh. But then the treasure belongs to the county . . ."

"It belongs to whoever finds it," Susan said firmly. "The county didn't bury it, some man did, and it says here that he probably died in the Civil War. Anyway, he never dug it up again, so we don't have to worry about *him* either."

"Well, I suppose it's all right, then," Victoria said.

"Sue, what's an H-bomb?" said Robert, pointing to another part of the page.

"Oh, never mind." She hastily folded up the paper and put it back in her pocket. "Come on, let's go."

"Have to find a stick first," Robert said. "For probing. Should be metal so it won't break."

Their searching finally uncovered a three-foot piece of brass curtain rod. Robert insisted on sharpening it; and the girls, hopping with impatience now, had to hold it across the manger while he scraped away with a file.

"Oh, come *on!*" Victoria said. "That's enough—the ground will be all soft with the rain anyway."

At last they were ready to start. Robert took the picnic hamper, Victoria held the probing rod, and Susan carried the spade.

"Now," Susan said when they reached the road. "Let's see . . ." She consulted the map, looked about her, and

shrugged her shoulders. "I guess the only thing to do is just walk down the lane and pretend I'm on Ward Street. If I can remember all the buildings and pace them off right, we'll end up pretty close. Your house is where the apartment building is"—'I hope,' she added privately. "So, here's the dry goods place next door . . . we'll just take a few steps for it, it's only a hole in the wall. Now the stationery place. Um. What's next? Oh, Wilson's Market, a lot of steps for that . . . Now the cigar store . . . and here's 95th! Isn't it wonderful, no traffic lights! Watch your step at the curb," she giggled.

"Where did you meet the old woman with the potatoes?" Victoria asked.

"Oh, down the road the other way—past Hollister's place."

"You'll have to show me some day, Sue. I want to put a marker there to remember all this by."

"A big stone," Robert said. " 'Sacred to the memory of Fortune-hunter Sweeney,' " he declaimed, " 'whose fate was decided—no, sealed, on this historic spot.' And hey, we could put dates on! 1960-1881: that'd make everybody sit up and wonder!"

"Don't say 'hey,' Bobbie."

"Stop talking a minute, will you?" Susan said. "I'm trying to think. Oh yes, Rumpelmayer's, that's a department store. It's huge, takes up almost half the block. Then there's a florist, I think—no, a bakery, and *then* the florist, and then a bank. Come on."

But when they reached what should have been—or was to be—94th Street, they were brought up short. Ward Lane angled off to the right here.

"Is this on the map?" Robert asked.

"No, Ward Street's supposed to be perfectly straight. Hmm. I think we'd better keep on in the same direction we've been going. That means we'll have to cut into the field."

But first the fence had to be negotiated: a split-rail zigzag fence, overgrown with honeysuckle and blackberry and sumac.

"Watch out for poison ivy. Remember when I had it last summer, Vic? I thought I was going to die!"

Victoria had become entangled with a blackberry runner, and was feeling uncharitable. "Serves you right," she sniffed. "Papa always said you didn't have to worry if you kept a sharp lookout."

"Well, I was looking for a bird's nest. You can't keep a sharp lookout everywhere at once. Ow! Look out, nettles."

The field seemed to be miles in extent. Some distance ahead of them stood a vast tree, with black-and-white cows lying in its shade.

"Won't they object to us being in their field?" Susan asked nervously.

"Oh no, we're friends," said Victoria. "Bobbie and I feed them apples in the fall."

It was rougher going now. The grass was hip-high and heavy with rain; walking through it was like wading in water. Their legs were soaked in an instant, and the damp heat made them sweat. Worst of all, Susan, now that she was off the road, forgot what buildings were supposed to be on this last and crucial block. Try as she might, she could conjure up no more than a vague memory of a red-brick insurance building and a jumble of show windows. In the end they had to guess the distance by compromising their three various notions of how much walking constituted a city block.

"Sharp left now," Susan said. They trudged a little further in silence.

"Well, whereabouts, Sue?" Robert asked.

She took out the map and looked at it helplessly. "I

don't know, it could be anywhere around here . . . Maybe there'll be a little hump over it. Or a hollow."

"You couldn't see a hump or hollow in this grass," Robert said. He thrust the rod into the ground. "Well, this isn't the place, anyway."

"We can't just go wandering around with that rod," Victoria said. "We'll miss some places and go over others twice."

"No, it's all right, Vic. Thing is to keep together. See the trail we make in the grass? We'll know where we've been. We'll go in a straight line and then double back right beside it."

"One thing, anyhow," Susan said. "The playground wasn't very big. It won't take long to cover it." She kept to herself the nagging suspicion that they weren't even on the playground—or what someday would be the playground.

They set out hopefully, keeping close together and trying to walk in a straight line. Robert jammed the rod into the ground at every step, grunting as he did so. It did not seem to Susan that the rod was penetrating very deeply.

"Thirty," said Victoria after a while.

"Thirty what?" Robert said, wiping his sleeve over his face.

"Thirty probes with the rod. I've been counting."

They looked back over the short way they had come, and then at the immensity of meadow all about them.

"Rome wasn't built in a day," Susan said faintly.

Twenty minutes later the rod grated against something.

"Here it is!" Robert shouted. "Give me the spade!"

He attacked the turf furiously. The earth was soft enough, but the grass roots were tough and thoroughly intertangled. There slowly came to light two pink worms and a small stone.

"Oh, pooh!" he groaned, flinging the spade down. "Here, one of you work the rod for a while. I'm done in."

An hour later they had dug up three more stones and a rusty plow point—to say nothing of worms, grubs, crickets, and other assorted specimens of soil life.

"I'm hungry," Robert said. "Let's eat."

"Oh, honestly!" Susan snapped, turning away.

"Isn't he impossible?" Victoria said.

"Well, who's doing most of the work? Look, I've got blisters on both hands! Even a horse would get fed by this time. All right, all right," he added feebly under their glares, "one more try."

They trudged off again, probing with the rod.

"OW!" Robert shrieked, soaring into the air like a kangaroo.

"What?" said Susan.

"Look out! Yellow jackets!"

"Run!" Victoria screamed.

Suddenly something that felt like a white-hot needle stabbed into Susan's leg. She screamed and fled. Another needle! She screamed again, and beat her arms about wildly. She never knew she could run so fast. For a tired and unfed treasure seeker, Robert was also doing superbly; while Victoria turned into a very deer, and outdistanced them both.

Puffing and blowing and rubbing their wounds, they gathered together at a safe distance from the humming nest. Only Victoria had gotten off unscathed. Susan had two stings, and Robert three.

"This is too much!" he said. "I don't care, *I'm* going to have something to eat. You two can suit yourselves. Let's get out of the sun a while, anyway."

They picked up their scattered tools and the picnic hamper, and headed wearily for the tree. The cows under it looked huge to Susan, and she began to drag her feet nervously; but Robert and Victoria made soothing noises of "Soo, boss boss, soo bossy," and the beasts merely looked on with mild interest as the three of them entered the shade and sat down.

"Wouldn't surprise me," Robert said gloomily, as he opened the hamper and fell to on the provender within, "if those yellow jackets weren't nesting right on the spot. Right in with the gold. Be just our luck."

Victoria groaned and rested her chin on her hands. "We might smoke them out," she suggested without conviction.

Susan was too discouraged to say anything. She sat down on a large flat rock and scuffed in the earth with her feet. Acorns were scattered all about in the litter. She picked up a few and rolled them between her fingers to feel their smoothness. Then, although she knew it would do no good, she took out the front page again.

FORTUNE FOUND AT CONSTRUCTION SITE

'Oh yes,' she thought savagely, 'it's all very well for Frank M. Zalewski. *He* had a bulldozer . . . Wish we did . . . Couldn't get it up the elevator, though. Some sort of electronic gadget? A what-do-you-call-it counter? No, they're only good for radioactive stuff. Is gold radioactive? Where would I get one anyway? Oh, golly, we'll *never* find it! How nice to be a cow . . . No worries; just lie in the sweet grass, looking into space, chewing, switching your tail . . .'

Hesitantly she put out her hand. The nearest cow licked it with a sandpapery tongue. The warm pressure of tears began to build up behind her eyelids. 'We'll never find it,' she thought again, 'we'll never find it.'

❧ 12 · CHANGING HISTORY ❧

"Ah!" said Robert, a considerable while later. "Well!" He rubbed his hands together in an offensively cheerful manner. "Shall we look some more?"

The girls stood up without a word and followed him into the field.

"Now, where were we?"

"Little further on," Susan sighed.

"More to the right, wasn't it?" said Victoria.

"Could've sworn we left off about here," Robert said minutes later. "Anybody hear the yellow jackets?"

"No," said Victoria. "We should be over *there*."

"Isn't this it?" said Susan a few minutes later. "What's happened to our trails, anyway?"

The meadow appeared everywhere as unruffled as it had when they first set foot on it. They looked at each other blankly as the realization came to them at last: there was no way of telling where they had already been. During their rest under the tree the grass had sprung erect again, obliterating all traces of their passing through earlier.

That was the last turn of the screw for Susan. She threw herself weeping to the ground. Robert and Victoria patted her back and dabbed at her face with their handkerchiefs, but it did no good; a conviction of the hopelessness of the whole undertaking crushed her. For her own sake she might not have minded so much; but she had as good as promised that the Walkers would be saved, and it was unbearable to have failed them so miserably. "It's just a wild goo-goose chase," she sobbed, "and it's all m-m-my fault, I wish I was *dead*."

When she had no tears left, Robert said gently, "Come on, Sue, don't give up yet. I'm not going to give up. Vic isn't either, are you, Vic?"

"No . . . At least, not if Sue doesn't."

"But I don't know where we are," Susan sniffled. "It's all just guessing. I don't know if your house is really where the apartment will be, and I don't know if we measured the blocks right or—or anything. I don't know *anything*." Her voice broke. She pulled her crumpled handkerchief from her pocket, and two acorns fell to the ground.

"Here," said Victoria, picking them up. "Don't cry any more, Sue." She gave an encouraging little smile. "You know what they say about acorns and oaks."

"Oaks?" Something stirred in Susan's mind.

" 'Great oaks from little acorns grow,' " Robert said. "It's something like Rome not being built in a day. It means don't get discour—"

"Wait a minute," Susan said. "Is that tree an *oak*?"

"Yes," said Victoria. "But what's that got to do with—?"

"Oh, how dumb can you get?" Susan exclaimed, smacking her forehead. "Of course it's an oak! Here I had these acorns right in my hand, and I never made the connection!"

"What connection?" said Robert.

"Acorns and oaks! Listen, do you know what they used to call the playground? *Oak Park!*"

"Ah!" Victoria said. "And that's the only oak tree for miles."

"So maybe we weren't so far off after all!"

"For that matter," Robert said thoughtfully, "it's the only real *landmark* for miles. You have to have a landmark when you bury something, if you want to find it again."

"That's right!" Victoria said. "Ninety paces due west from the old oak! Or south—"

"Or east or north—or any point between. Or any number of paces, for that matter. Thunderation! I wish we had *his* map instead of the news—"

"Listen!" Susan cried, seizing them both so suddenly that they jumped. "What if you were going to bury something and you didn't want to fool with any map?"

"Well," Robert stammered, "you—you could write down the number of paces and the direction."

"No, no!—too dangerous—somebody might find your note. No notes, no maps! Think!"

"You could just remember how many paces—" Victoria offered hopefully.

"No!" Susan shouted. "Why try to remember anything? You'd do the simplest thing you could think of! *You'd bury it right under the tree!*"

A shocked second of silence.

Robert whispered, "That must be it!"

"Come on!"

How they ran! The great yellow jacket escape was nothing compared to this sprint. "Boo!" Robert yelled at the cows. "Yah yah! Yoo *hooooop!*" The animals snorted and heaved themselves upright and shied away.

"Spade!" Robert panted. "Give me the spade!"

"*Wait* a minute," Victoria said. "We ought to—"

Robert stabbed the spade into the ground with all his strength. "Here!" he shouted. "Something solid! No rock, either!" The crumbly leaf mould gave way as easily as sand under his attack. "There it is—it's wood!" He rammed the corner of the spade against the dark surface. It glanced off, leaving a moist white wound.

"It's only a root," Victoria said. "Now be sensible, Bobbie. We'll only wear ourselves out digging at random this way."

"I guess it doesn't matter where we start," Susan said faintly as she looked about. "Under the tree" had sounded simple enough when she said it, but now she saw that the words could mean anywhere in an area of hundreds of square feet—or possibly (it was a huge tree) thousands of square feet . . .

"It might matter," Victoria said. "Now, if *I* were burying something I wanted to find again, I'd pick some sort of mark on the trunk and dig by that."

They circled the tree slowly, studying every foot of trunk.

"That bump is the only real mark," Robert said.

"Except for that smooth place," said Susan, pointing.

"That's just where the cows rub themselves—it might not have been there when the man buried the money."

Susan gazed up into the branches. "Know what I'd do? I'd pick the biggest branch and dig under it. Which is the biggest—this one or that one?"

"This one," said Victoria. "I think."

"Look!" Robert said. "That one's got a crook in it! That's where I'd dig, right under the crook. You couldn't possibly miss a mark like that."

"Well, you couldn't miss the bump on the trunk, either. One's just as good as the other."

"No it isn't, Vic. You can dig right *under* the crook, but you can see the bump anywhere from here on out."

"We'll have to try everything," Susan sighed. "Anything could be a mark, actually. The thing is, we'll have to be systematic about it."

"Around and around," said Robert. "Bigger circles each time. Let's start under the crook, though—just in case."

"How about roots?" Victoria asked. "The ground will be full of them."

"That's all right," said Susan. "Every time the rod hits something we'll mark the place with an acorn. Then if we end up with a line of acorns we'll know there's a root underneath, and we won't have to dig there."

"That means we'll have to pick up all the acorns first," Robert said dubiously. "So we won't mix up the markers and the other ones."

"There must be millions of them," Victoria murmured, scanning the ground.

At that instant Susan gave a shriek and jumped.

"It's only a cow, Sue," Robert said. "It won't hurt you."

"Well, why does it have to sneak up from behind and blow in my ear?"

"Just curious. Oh, thunderation!" he went on angrily. "Here come the rest of them. How are we going to keep track of where we've probed with *them* trampling around and lying down on top of everything? You can't *keep* a cow out of the shade on a day like this. They just keep coming back as fast as you chase them."

Susan quavered. Her legs were shaking with the fright the cow had given her, and despair was closing in again. Under the tree, indeed! They were no better off than before. She was going to cry again . . .

Blindly she turned away and sank down on her former seat.

"The rock!" Victoria cried.

"What?"

"Under the rock!"

"Come on!" Robert shouted.

"But—but—" Susan stammered as they yanked her to her feet and turned her around.

"Got your fingers under?"

"Grab that edge!"

"Ready? Heave!"

"Heave!"

The rock was large and flat and heavy, but it stirred slightly. Three small grey furry things darted out from under.

"Ooh!" Victoria squeaked. She let go her grip and jumped back. The rock fell.

"They're only mice," Robert said disgustedly.

"I don't like them running over my feet. If you don't *mind*."

"Did you hear how the rock fell?" Susan whispered. "It sounded hollow underneath!"

"Oh, come *on*, Vic!"

"Got it?"

"Heave! Heave!"

Their legs and arms trembled, their spines cracked. The rock suddenly tore away from its bed, and lifted, and toppled over. The earth underneath was criss-crossed with mouse tunnels.

"It sounded hollow," Susan insisted. "Listen!" She stamped on the bare earth. "There! Did you hear that?" She stamped again, harder, with the point of her heel. There was a soft, punky, crushing noise. Her foot vanished. Something clinked as she pulled it out of the hole.

They dropped to their knees, plunged their hands into the hole, and brought them up heavy with slithers of coins. "Oh!" they breathed, "ah!" as they let the golden eagles sift through their fingers with a slide and a clink and a glitter . . .

"Let's count them!" Robert said.

"No!" said Susan, suddenly dropping her handful and straightening up. "We must be crazy! Right out in the open, where anybody that wants to can come along and see us! Let's cover it up, quick! We can come back and get it tonight after dark."

Her panic was infectious. They all jumped up and looked about them. Except for themselves and the cows the world appeared empty of life; but at any moment—"Come on!" said Robert. They struggled and grunted until the stone was back in place, settled it down as naturally as they could and brushed the grass and fallen oak leaves around its edges. Then they dropped down at full length and relaxed again, letting a quiet gloating feeling take possession of them. There was a long silence. The cows drifted back into the shade, one by one, swishing their tails.

"I'm hungry!" Victoria suddenly announced. "How about you, Sue?"

"Oh, yes!" said Susan, suddenly rediscovering an appetite that she had thought was lost forever.

"Listen—" Robert began uneasily.

But Victoria had already found out. "Robert, you *hog*! You didn't leave a thing! Oh, you—you *Bobolink*!"

"Well," he protested, dodging out of her reach, "I kept offering you some. You wouldn't even *listen*. What's a fellow supposed to do, anyway? Waste it all? Here, you can have these. I was saving them for later on."

So the girls had to make do with three rather battered sandwiches from his pockets.

"I wish we could've counted it," Robert said, when it seemed safe to speak again.

"Good thing gold isn't edible," Victoria sniffed, "or there wouldn't be any *left* to count."

"All right, all right. I said I was sorry, didn't I?"

"No, you didn't."

"Well, I am, so there . . . I still wish we could count it. How much does the paper say, Sue?"

"Sixty thousand."

"Sixty thousand!" he whistled. "You know what, that's a huge amount to leave for the twentieth century . . . Come to think of it, why should we leave any? Are you sure it's that much?"

"See for yourself," she said, giving him the front page.

Robert unfolded it, looked at it, turned it over, turned it over again, and said, "Wrong page, Sue."

"It can't be—I only had one."

"You sure?"

"Well of course I'm sure! I just tore off one page."

"Great Caesar! Look—it's—it's *different*!"

Susan felt her scalp tingle as she examined the page. Most of it was exactly as before. But the headline was now

MAYOR ASKS BOND ISSUE FOR WATER

In the column where the treasure story had been there was an account of a press conference at City Hall. The map now showed the whole city, with three black X's distributed over it; and the caption said, "New Reservoir Sites Proposed By City Engineers."

"You know what?" Victoria whispered after a while. "They never found the treasure in the twentieth century after all!"

"But they *did*," Susan said. "That's why it was in the paper."

"But it's not in the paper any more. It won't be in the paper. It's just as Bobbie said—if *we* find it they *can't*."

"Yes, but—" Susan began. She appealed helplessly to Robert. "What does it mean?"

"Well," he said, rubbing his head slowly with both hands. "I guess it means that they *did* find it until you came up the elevator and *we* found it, and from then on they *didn't* find it. If that makes any sense."

"That's it," Victoria said in awe-stricken tones. "Do you know what we've done? *We've changed history!*"

"Which means we don't have to leave any for the twentieth century after all," Robert said. "When we come back for it tonight we can take every last penny of it."

⚡ 13 · NIGHT ALARMS, ⚡ MORNING THOUGHTS

"No!" Victoria said. "It would show through the water. What we should do is bury it in the garden somewhere."

"Trouble with that," Robert said, "is that I'd have to do the digging. It'll be all right in the pond, Vic—the water isn't clear enough to show anything on the bottom."

"But then one of us would have to get all wet pulling it out again."

"Well, *I* don't mind getting wet."

"And besides, a lot of it could get lost in the mud. You know how deep it is."

"Well, I guess it is pretty deep . . . What do you think, Sue?"

But Susan wasn't listening. Every muscle she had ached, her eyes were gritty from lack of sleep, but she was filled with a dreamy, yearning kind of happiness. She lay in the grass with her hands under her head and gazed up at the Milky Way. Victoria and Robert rested in the dark beside her, their backs propped against a wheelbarrow. In the wheelbarrow lay a potato sack, bulging with gold pieces. Crickets trilled and rustled about them.

A nearby cow worked through the grass with a juicy crunching rhythm.

"Sue?"

"Mm?"

"Where are we going to hide the treasure when we get home?"

"I don't care," she murmured.

"You have to care, Sue. It's your treasure."

"No, it belongs to all of us. You did as much work as I did."

"He's right, though, Sue," Victoria said. "If it weren't for you we'd never—"

"Oh, be sensible! What could *I* do with it? I can't take the time to spend it here, and there's no use taking it to the twentieth century because they don't use gold money any more—it's illegal or something. I couldn't carry it anyway. And why do we have to hide it? We'll just give it to your Mama. That's why we dug it up in the first place."

"I don't know how we're *ever* going to thank you," Victoria said.

"Oh, nonsense," Susan said. "I don't want any thanks. I just want to look at the stars for a while."

There was a long silence.

"Sue?" Victoria said.

"Mm?"

"I've just been thinking . . . How are you going to give it to Mama? Are you going to tell her about—everything?"

"Goodness, no! All that explaining? It's going to be hard enough just to explain to my own father where I've been and what I've been doing."

"Well, how, then?"

"I don't know, I haven't thought about it. Just leave it on the doorstep, I guess. What do you think?"

"Well," Victoria said slowly, "I don't know if that's the best way . . . It'd be a dreadful shock to Mama. I mean—

sixty thousand dollars out of the clear blue sky! How are we ever going to make her believe that it's really for *her*?"

"We can pretend it's from a rich uncle in Australia," Robert said.

"Oh, pooh! You know perfectly well we haven't got any uncles in Australia."

"I see your point, though," Susan said. "Hmmm . . . How about giving her just a little to begin with? Anybody can believe in a *hundred* dollars, can't they?"

"I know!" said Robert. "There can be a note with it that says, 'From the Mysterious Stranger'!"

"How about 'From a Well-Wisher'?" Susan suggested.

"That's it!" Victoria cried. " 'Do not despair,' it'll say. 'To dash the tear from your cheek, to make the smile appear—no, bloom—to make the smile bloom on your lips has ever been the—wish?—no, make it desire—ever been the desire of' and then we sign it 'One who wishes you well.' "

" 'More to follow,' " Robert added. "Just to prepare her for the rest. Sue'll have to do it, though, Mama knows our handwriting. Will you, Sue?"

"Sure."

"How romantic!" Victoria sighed. "Mama will be so mystified! She probably will think it's from some distinguished gentleman with grey hair who's been hopelessly in love with her ever since he saw her in the park one day when she was but a girl."

"Oh—listen—to—*that*!" Robert groaned.

"You're an unfeeling brute, that's what you are. The only thing *you* can get sentimental about is *food*."

There was another silence.

"Anyway," Robert said at last, "we're right back where we started. If we're going to give Mama a little bit at a time we still have to hide the rest somewhere."

"All right," Victoria sighed. "Anywhere but the pond."

"Anything but digging another hole, too. What do you think, Sue?—Sue?"

"Oh, good grief!" Susan said. An idea was struggling to be born in her mind, but how could she think with all this talk going on? She stood up and stretched her aching arms. "I don't care. How about the stable? Couldn't we just hide it under the straw?"

"Hey!" said Robert. "That's it. Why didn't I think of—"

"Well, let's go then," Susan said. And then, to make up for the shortness of her tone, she added, "It must be getting awfully late."

The Walkers got up groaning. Robert took the shafts of the wheelbarrow in his grip and heaved upward with a terrific grunt.

"Oh, no! It must weigh a *ton*—I can hardly budge it."

"You take one handle and I'll take the other," Susan said. "Then Vicky, when one of us gets tired."

They soon discovered that the wheelbarrow was more easily pulled than pushed; but they were worn out, and it was too dark to pick the best way across the field, so that even with two of them pulling they could not proceed more than a hundred feet at a time. It look them nearly an hour to reach the far corner of the field, where there was a gate that opened on Ward Lane.

"At least," Robert panted, "it'll roll easier on the road."

It did. Now they could go several hundred feet before stopping to rest and trade off places. But when they had covered only half the distance between the gate and the Walkers' house, the wheel of the barrow began to chirp. Each chirp grew louder and longer, until the "*weeeet weeeet weeeet*" was almost continuous.

"Stop, stop!" Susan cried. "I can't stand it. It's worse than fingernails on a blackboard."

"That'll wake up everybody at our house and Hollister's too," Robert said. "Why didn't I think of oiling the—"

"Listen!"

They froze. Susan, straining her ears, could hear a faint rhythmic sound far down the lane.

"We've got to hide!" Robert muttered. "That bush—" He ran to a looming shadow by the roadside, rustled about in it, and came hurrying back. "All right—no thorns. Ram the wheelbarrow right into it."

"Weeeeeeet!" shrieked the wheel. The bush crackled and snapped like a falling tree. "Get behind!" Robert whispered. "Down! Hug the ground!"

They lay with their faces pressed into the weeds, scarcely daring to breathe. 'Good night!' Susan thought; 'nobody could have missed hearing that!' The sound came steadily on toward them, resolving, as it grew louder, into the clopping of hooves, the singing crunch of wheels, the creak of harness. Louder and still louder, until it was upon them, a shadow horse, a shadow buggy, a shadow driver huddled on the seat; the horse whickered softly, the huddled figure snored; and they were past, melting again into the dark, clop clop rumble and creak.

"Asleep," Robert breathed. "We're in luck!"

"Asleep!" Susan said in a shocked voice.

"Why not?" said Victoria. "The horse knows the way home."

"I'm going to go get an oil can," Robert said. "If you two stay quiet behind the bush you'll be all right."

"Well . . ." said Victoria.

"Has to be done, Vic—we can't let the wheel make all that noise without waking everybody up."

"Oh . . . all right. But *please* hurry, Bobbie, and—and do take care."

"Oh, girls!" he grumbled. "You'd think I was going through the enemy lines or something . . ." His voice faded in the dark.

Susan edged closer to Victoria, trying to make it appear

as if her real intention were to get comfortable. Somehow the night was not as beautiful as it had been. The shadows seemed blacker all of a sudden, and sinister in shape; yet the one they were sitting in did not hide them very well. The pale oval that was Victoria's face stood out much too clearly.

At the end of ten minutes Victoria whispered shakily, "Sue? Do you—do you believe in ghosts?"

"No!" said Susan, much more loudly than she had intended. They both jumped, then cowered with hearts thudding. "No," she whispered.

"Neither do I—in the daytime."

"Stop it. It's all nonsense."

"Maggie said she saw her brother once seven months after he was drowned at sea! There was seaweed in his hair and his face was all blue—"

"*Stop* it."

Five minutes later Victoria whispered, "I wish Bobbie would hurry."

"So do I."

"What if something happened to him? What if he met a *tramp?*"

"Will you *please* stop that?" Susan whispered.

"I can't help it," Victoria moaned. "He's been gone much too long, and there *are* tramps on the road—"

"Listen!"

Footsteps were approaching in the dark. Robert—or someone else? They clutched each other, suffocating with terror.

A light bloomed on the road. Behind it a voice shakily enquired, "Vic? Sue?"

"Bobbie!" they screamed. They were up and running. The bull's-eye lantern winked out, and Robert's white face loomed out of the dark. Susan screamed again and went sprawling.

"Sue! What's the matter? Sue?" They fluttered anxiously around her.

"Ankle," she sobbed. "Oh, oh . . ."

"Which one?" The bull's-eye winked on again.

"Left one. Ow! Don't pinch it!"

"Oh, Sue, I am sorry."

"Think you can stand on it?"

"No," she wept. "Can't even wiggle it."

"Wheelbarrow!" Robert said. "It's all right, Sue, we'll get you home. Just let me oil the wheel."

The barrow was trundled out, its wheel lubricated, and Susan hoisted on board. Victoria and Robert took the handles, struggled a few feet, narrowly avoided a tip-over, and collapsed.

"Too heavy!" Robert gasped. "We'll never do it."

"One thing after another," Victoria quavered, wringing her hands. "What're we going to *do*?"

"Dump me off," said Susan. "I can hide under the bush again. Take the treasure home and then come back for me."

"Leave you here *alone*?" Victoria cried. "Never!"

"It's all right, Vicky, I can—"

"No!"

"All right, then, we'll have to leave the treasure here and take *me* home."

There was a glum silence.

"Well, come on!" she cried. The throbbing of her ankle made her savage. "Me or it. We can't stand around all night making up our minds."

"I know!" Robert said. "We can hide it in the fence-row." He opened the shutter of his bull's-eye, went over to the fence, and began to explore along the overgrowth. "Here we are! The blackberry runners make a kind of tunnel. Plenty of dead leaves to bury it under, too."

"Don't forget to keep some out for your Mama," Susan said.

Robert and Victoria had an exasperating time of it, struggling with the weight of the gold, and getting ripped by thorns at every move. They were not speaking to each other by the time they were through. Susan, wrapped in her pain, had nothing further to say either. The long journey back seemed more like the retreat of a beaten army than the triumphant home-coming of successful treasure hunters.

Carrying Susan up to Victoria's room was out of the question. Robert fetched a blanket, and Susan was bedded down in the stable on the very pile of straw that was to have hidden the treasure.

She was awakened in the morning by a fly running over her face. She did not open her eyes at once, but lay there for a while, warm, drowsy and comfortable, thinking how nice it was not to have to worry for once about the Genial Host and his screaming audience. She could loll there until she was *ready* to get up . . . Still, she would have to go back today—there was no longer any excuse for staying. Ankle? She wiggled her foot cautiously. Still painful, but much better; she'd be able to hobble on it, anyway.

No excuse for staying.

She sighed, and opened her eyes.

There had been a heavy dew-fall during the night, or perhaps another shower of rain. The weeds and grasses by the stable door were covered with drops, all adazzle in the slanting sun. What she could see of the sky was covered with little quilted clouds. They had a pearly glow as if each bore its own light within it. Hollister's chickens clucked and crooned in the distance, other bird voices

were raised in various song. A small spot detached itself from the lintel, dropped, paused, hung in mid-air silhouetted against the clouds, dropped and paused again; 'a spider,' Susan thought; 'Charlotte, making Charlotte's web!' A swallow shot through the doorway, arced upward as if to burst through the roof, checked, turned, darted out into the sunlight again like a small blue explosion. Charlotte dropped three more inches and waved her legs. Susan's heart filled; she sucked in her breath. The thought she had been struggling with last night was sharp and clear in her mind.

She wanted to live here.

Well?

No excuse for staying; she *had* to go back. And yet . . . And yet . . .

She was still deep in thought an hour later when Victoria burst in.

"Sue! How's your poor ankle?"

"Hi, Vicky. Still hurts, but I think I can walk on it."

"Good! I'm so glad! Wasn't it a nightmare last night? They never tell you about these things in stories—the people find the gold and live happily ever after—no mention of having to hide from people and being frightened out of your wits and spraining ankles. Or being so stiff you can hardly move next day."

"Oh, well, everything's all right now."

"I wish I could think so! You know, Bobbie and I simply didn't have the strength to go back after the treasure last night. It's still in the brambles!"

"Oh? Well, it's hidden, isn't it?"

"Oh, yes, it's hidden all right—leaves all over it and brambles in front of the leaves. But I'm not going to feel safe until we get it home."

"You did remember to take some for your Mama, didn't you?"

"Yes, Bobbie's got it, twelve eagles. But we can't do anything until we have the note. So could you please?" Victoria drew a sheet of note paper and a pencil from her pocket.

Susan had not cared much last night for the idea of dashing tears from cheeks and making smiles bloom; and now, before Victoria could mention them again, she scribbled, "Do not depair. From a well-wisher. More to follow." "There!" she said. "Now, I have to go back."

Victoria's face fell. "Oh, *Sue*—"

"Now wait a minute. I've got one more trip here, and I've—well, I've been thinking . . ." Suddenly the enormity of what she had been thinking struck her, and she broke off, chewing her knuckle and staring at Victoria's waiting face. "Well," she went on lamely, "it's probably crazy . . ."

"*Nothing* you think of is crazy. Please tell me!"

Susan, with some hesitation, told her.

"Oh!" Victoria breathed. "How romantic! Oh, Sue!"

"It's going to take some doing . . ."

"*You* can do *anything!* Are you going right now?"

"Yes, if you can keep them all away from the elevator for a while."

"All right! Let's see. I know, I'll pretend I just found the money and the note on the front doorstep. Mama usually goes into the sun parlor when there's a crisis, and I can have Bobbie bring Maggie in, and then I'll wave my handkerchief—come here, I'll show you."

She pulled Susan to her feet and supported her while she limped to the door.

"Can you manage?"

"It's all right. It just twinges when I put my weight on it."

"Don't go out! Just put your head around the door.

There, do you see that row of windows? That's it. I'll wave my handkerchief out of the one to the far left."

"Got it. Oh! The picture."

"That's right, I forgot. How about a locket?"

"Perfect!"

"All right. I'll leave it on the table across from the elevator. Anything else?"

"No, I can't think of anything else."

"Well . . . good luck, Sue."

"It isn't luck so much," said Susan, "as management."

"*I* know."

They exchanged a secret smile. Victoria squeezed Susan's hands and left her. Susan, her mind churning, her heart pounding, her stomach quivering with excitement, waited . . . waited . . . waited . . . Ah! There was the signal! She hobbled from the stable as fast as she could for the back door, the elevator, and the twentieth century.

❧ 14 · MR. SHAW HUMORS ❧ HIS DAUGHTER

There was a long silence when Susan finished recounting her adventures. Mr. Shaw's expression was one of incredulity, bafflement, concern, and even fear. He stared at her, twisting his hands slowly in his lap.

"I knew you'd find it hard to believe," she sighed.

"Fantastic!" he murmured. "Fan*tas*tic!"

"Well, I know it sounds that way, Daddy, but it's all true just the same."

"I don't know, chick, I don't know. You . . ."

"I what?"

"Well, you've always had a vivid imagination. Now don't misunderstand me! I think imagination is a fine thing, and I've always been glad that yours—"

"Oh, Daddy," Susan said reproachfully, "you don't think I'm making it up, do you?"

"Well, Susie—old women with potatoes! 1881! Buried treasure!" He waved his hands. "Suppose *I* disappeared for three days and came back with a rigamarole like that, would *you* believe it? Now, I'm not for a minute implying that you're deliberately trying to deceive me."

"What are you implying, then?"

"Well," he said cautiously, "I think you've had a—a shock of some kind."

"Like what, for instance?"

"*I* don't know, chick—that's what I'm trying to find out. You're the only one who can tell me."

"I've *been* telling you, Daddy. I've told you every single thing that's happened to me."

Mr. Shaw gently shook his head. "I'm afraid it's all hallucinations, Susie. I know they can seem very real for a while, until you think them over."

"Look at my clothes," she demanded. "Are they hallucinations? Look," pulling down her stocking, "yellow jacket stings, two of them! Could I make *those* up in my head?"

"Well, the clothes are real enough," he admitted, "and those certainly look like bites or stings of some kind . . ."

"Well?"

"So there must be some explanation."

"Of *course* there is—what have I been telling you—?"

"No, no, Susie—I mean a *real* explanation."

"Oh, good grief! Here," she said, taking an eagle out of her pocket. "Is *this* an hallucination?"

"Where did you get *that?*"

"Oh, honestly!" she cried in despair. "Toby, what can we *do* with him?"

Toby gazed up from her lap with slitted eyes, and purred.

"Well, chick," Mr. Shaw said hesitantly, after turning the coin over in his hands for a time, "this is all . . . Look, I have an idea. Let's go and see a doctor. Anyone you want—some nice kind understanding man. Just to talk things over?"

Tears of vexation spurted to her eyes. "No," she wept. "What good will talking to anybody else do if my own *father* won't believe me?"

"Oh, Susie," he said, hugging her tight, "don't cry, don't cry. I'm sorry, honey. I don't want to fight with you. I'd really like to believe you, you know. It's just that . . ."

Suddenly she saw the way.

"Daddy," she murmured against his vest, "will you promise me something? Just one little easy thing?"

"Sure, chick. What is it?"

"Will you go up in the elevator with me? Just once?"

She felt him stiffen a little. "Why?" he asked cautiously.

"So you can see for yourself."

"But, Susie, we've been in the elevator together hundreds of times."

"We never went to the top together."

"But there's nothing to see at the top—"

"*Please,* Daddy. Just once? Just to humor me?"

"Oh, all right," he sighed. "I guess it can't do any harm."

"Promise? Cross your heart and hope to die?"

"It's a promise. Want to go now?"

"No, I want to talk with you about something else first."

"All right." He sat down again, still looking at her a little warily. "Fire away."

She chewed her knuckle for a moment, wondering how to begin. "Now this is serious, Daddy, extremely serious. I can't stand it if you laugh or anything."

"I'll be solemn as a judge! Go on."

"Well," she said, blushing, "it's just an idea I had . . . I—I think you ought to get married again."

"Oh my!" he cried, throwing up his hands in mock despair. "Do I detect Mrs. Clutchett's hand in all this?"

"She's got nothing to do with it. Why do you mention her?"

"Because getting me married again has been her constant and unwearying idea for the last year. Whenever she can get me alone she talks of nothing else."

"Well, she's perfectly right, then. Why not?"

"I know, chick, I know—don't bite my head off. She *is* right, I guess. So are you. But . . . Well, how can I explain it?" He thought for a moment, and continued, "You see, sometimes when a person has loved another person very much, and the other person dies . . . well, sometimes it's very hard to get interested in anyone else. Or even to think about it—"

"Oh," she interrupted impatiently, "that's just what Mrs. Walker said. My goodness, why can't parents be sensible? Look, I loved Mother just as much as you did, but that doesn't mean I have to—well, just scrooge up inside myself and never love anyone else again. Never even *try*."

Now it was Mr. Shaw's turn to blush.

"Honestly, Daddy, I know how you feel. Really I do. I suppose it's natural to feel that way for a year or so, but not for*ever*."

"Well," he said with an embarrassed laugh. "I guess I stand corrected . . . May I ask what brought all this up?"

"I just want to have a Mama again, that's all."

"Just any Mama?"

"No-o-o, not exactly."

"Aha!" he teased, "I thought not. I know that look in your eye! I'll bet you've got a candidate all picked out, haven't you?"

"Yes," she giggled. "That's why we're going up in the elevator—you promised, now!"

"Oh? Someone on the seventh floor?"

"No—Mrs. Walker."

"Who?"

"Mrs. *Walker*. The lady I've been telling you about."

Mr. Shaw leaned back and closed his eyes. "Now wait a minute," he said faintly. "Wait a minute. Let me get this straight. This dream of yours seems so real that you are not only proposing to take me into it, you are also proposing that I should get *married* in it? Is that it?"

"That's it," she said cheerfully. "Now please don't look at me that way, Daddy, the idea will seem perfectly sensible as soon as you get used to it."

Mr. Shaw rubbed his face and groaned.

"Well, I can't *make* you believe me," she sighed; "you'll just have to see for yourself. It'll be simple. We'll go up late at night, and sneak out of the house, and spend the night in the stable. Vicky's going to smuggle blankets and pillows out there for us, and Bobbie'll see that we have something to eat. And then next morning we'll just stroll up to the Hollisters' and ask for room and board. You can tell them that you're vacationing and that some friend recommended the country hereabouts, and that you've already sent the trap back to the—well, I'll coach you in all that. Then I'll pretend to make Vicky's acquaintance—of course she wants to see you before she gives her final approval, but that's nothing to worry about. And then we'll introduce you to Mrs. Walker, and then—well, then the inevitable will happen. You don't have to worry about a thing, Daddy, you are awfully handsome, you know. And you'll be rich, too!"

"Incredible," Mr. Shaw said. "Incredible."

"Well, aren't you going to thank me? I'm giving up my career for you!"

"Your what?"

"My stage career. I'm sure I won't be able to go on the stage when we're there. It wasn't respectable in those days, was it? I think I read something about it once. I'm just teasing, though. Really I'm being very selfish. I want to live in a big house, and I want to live out in the country where it's so quiet and pretty, with birds singing and all those stars at night and room for everybody and sweet-smelling air. I want to wear long dresses that go *swish*, when I grow up, and big flowery hats. I want a brother and a sister to play with and fight with and have secrets with. And most of all I want a Mama like Mrs. Walker—I want *her*, I mean. Daddy, she's so beautiful you won't believe it! I only saw her once, and I love her as much as I love you, only in a different way, of course. And she's good, and—I don't know. I want to be like her when I grow up . . . Look, here's a picture of her. It doesn't really do her justice, but it gives you some idea."

She gave Victoria's locket to her father.

"And you know, Daddy, if the inevitable *isn't*—well, inevitable, we can always come back. But if we do come back it'll be for always, because this is the last trip I'm allowed."

There was a long silence while he studied the picture. "That," he said at last, "is a lovely woman. Where did you get this, Susie?"

She could see that there was no use insisting on the truth of the matter. "Oh, never mind," she sighed. "You don't have to believe me, Daddy, it doesn't really matter. The main thing is going up the elevator, that's all I really care about right now. You did promise me that."

"Yes."

"Tonight?" she insisted.

"Yes, tonight."

"Good! Let's have some breakfast, and then I want to go out and buy a diary like Vicky's. Oh, I almost forgot! We'll have to get you a costume."

"A *what*?"

"A nineteenth century suit. Now don't *look* like that, Daddy, I'll get it with my own money."

"But whatever for?"

"To wear when we go up the elevator."

"Now wait a minute!" Mr. Shaw said, slapping his

knee. "This is too much! I promised I'd go up the elevator with you, and I will. But I will *not* make a fool of myself by getting into fancy dress to do it!"

"But, Daddy—"

"No!"

"But, Daddy, you can't go into the nineteenth century with twentieth century clothes on! It'll spoil everything!"

"We're not *going* to the nineteenth century!"

"Well, then, do it—just to humor me."

"Oh, Susie, don't cry—I can't stand it! All right, all right, all right—*on one condition*."

"What?"

"You'll have to promise me that the *minute* we come back from this—this masquerade, you'll come with me to see a doctor."

"You mean a psychiatrist, don't you?"

"No use pussyfooting with you, is there?" he said wanly. "Yes, I mean a psychiatrist."

"All right," she said, smiling again. "*If* we come back I'll go see anyone you want. I'll cooperate one hundred percent. You can even make the appointment now, if you want."

He looked so relieved and hopeful that her heart went out to him. "Poor Daddy," she murmured, kissing him. "You're in for an awful shock, I'm afraid. But you're going to love it when you get used to it."

☙ 15 · AN OLD PHOTOGRAPH ☙

I heard Susan's story from Mrs. Clutchett that afternoon. In retelling it I have supplied many details, but have changed nothing essential. Mrs. Clutchett heard the whole thing by simply and frankly eavesdropping. The good woman had thought herself entitled to some explanation, after having stayed by Mr. Shaw's side night and day since Wednesday; so as soon as she had shut the bedroom door on Susan and Mr. Shaw, she knelt down and applied herself to the keyhole. Like a tape recorder, her ear soaked up and permanently stored everything Susan had said; and, again like a tape recorder, she faithfully relayed it all to me.

She didn't believe a word of it.

"1881!" she snorted. "Did you ever hear such raving nonsense in your life? Now, the minute I saw that poor child step out of the elevator this morning, I said to myself, 'Well! if ever I've seen hysteria, *this is it.*' Oh, that smile of hers didn't fool me for a minute. I've seen shock before, that's just the way it takes people sometimes. Why, poor Mr. Clutchett was hit on the head once by a boxful of old magazines and went around for hours with such a smile you'd think somebody'd given him a hundred dollars; but it was just daze all the time. Now, if you ask me, that story is pure invention. What's *really* bothering people always comes out in the end. All you have to do is be patient and wait, and the story behind the story comes out."

She fixed me with a significant look and pursed her lips.

"All right," I said, "what was the real story?"

"Asking her father to marry again!" she cried triumphantly. "What did I tell you just the other day! Did you mark my words? Wasn't I telling you the pure gospel, believe it or not? Here that poor motherless lamb had it bottled up inside her until she had to run away and make up this *fantastic* story just to try to convince Mr. Shaw how important it was to her."

"Wait a minute," I said. "How about her dress? You said she was wearing an old-fashioned dress."

"Why, that's nothing! She was always playing these parts in plays. I saw her myself last year at the school. She was so *natural* up there on the stage, it took my breath away. No sir, she could get any kind of costume she wanted at school. It was all just part of the hysteria."

I didn't know what to believe myself. Susan, although I'd only seen her a few times, hadn't struck me as the hysterical sort. Still, there was plenty of evidence that she had a vivid imagination; and something might have happened to unbalance it temporarily. Her story was certainly queer enough. I wanted to hear it again from Susan herself; but I had no right to ask her to tell it, and doubtless her father's disbelief would make her shy about discussing her experiences with a comparative stranger. The only thing to do, then, was to make what investigations I could on my own.

So as soon as Mrs. Clutchett left my apartment (with a sniff at its disorder, and a promise to set me to rights next week), I took a trip in the elevator. Not having met the old woman with the potatoes and the fly-away hat, I expected nothing of this venture—and nothing was the result of it. The elevator laboriously carried me to the seventh floor and stopped.

Next, I went down to the basement to check up on the week's newspapers. I expected nothing to come of this, either. If Susan and Robert and Victoria *had* changed history—which was ridiculous on the face of it—the front pages of each and every newspaper for Wednesday would be changed, and there would be no mention of treasure; and if Susan were making the whole thing up, there would still be no mention of treasure. But the idea must have come from somewhere, so I went through Mr. Bodoni's stack of papers to see what I could find. MAYOR ASKS BOND ISSUE FOR WATER was the big local news for Wednesday. There was no mention whatever of the 93rd Street playground. I did find a copy of that day's paper with the front page torn off; but there could be more than one explanation for that.

So it was with a feeling of going on a fool's errand that I walked up to the 93rd Street playground next Monday morning. Construction was indeed going on there. There was no playground any more, only a vast hole fenced off with boards and full of the Delta-Schirmerhorn Construction Company's machinery. I went into the foreman's shack. The foreman himself was seated behind a table, yelling into a telephone, while a short, stocky workman stood by with a yellow slip in his hand.

"Iron pipe!" the foreman was bellowing. "Six-inch iron pipe! All right, what's this four-inch plastic stuff doing here? No it doesn't. Look at the specs again, for Pete's sake! I don't care, get it here right now! Look, I got a whole crew of plumbers here sitting around and drawing pay for nothing. Don't gimme that! Get that pipe here!"

He slammed the phone down and growled, "What d'*you* want?"

"Sorry to bother you," I said. "I was just wondering if you found anything out of the ordinary when you were bulldozing here last week."

"Nah; dirt, stones, tree roots—usual stuff. Smatter, you lose something?"

"No, I—ah—just wondering. Thanks."

He seized the yellow slip out of the other man's hand, looked at it incredulously, and began screaming into the phone again. It seemed like an excellent time to get out. As I was leaving, the other man hurried out after me, calling, "Hey, Mac!"

"Yes?"

"What didja have in mind? Like finding something, maybe?"

"Oh, in a way," I said, feeling like an idiot. "I just had an idea that maybe this ground had never been dug up before—you know."

"Yeah? C'mere a minute."

He beckoned me around the shack to a private spot.

"Matter a fact, I found something here last Wednesday. I'm a 'dozer operator, see? I always keep my eye open. Ya never know what the blade's gonna turn up. Get a load of this."

From his pocket he produced a gold coin.

It was a shock to see it—a pleasurable shock. I suddenly realized that I had wanted to believe Susan all along.

"At's a collector's item, betcha anything," he gloated. "1862, it says on it. Hey, you a dealer? Wanna make me an offer?"

"No, thanks," I said. "I couldn't even afford it at par. Thanks for showing me, anyway." It seemed wiser not to mention that if three children had not gotten there first he would now have thousands of collector's items instead of just one.

'I'll have to see Susan tonight,' I thought. 'She might like to know that at least one person believes her.'

When I arrived at the Shaws' apartment that evening I found it occupied by an exasperated Detective Haugen, a tearful Mrs. Clutchett, and a bewildered Mr. Bodoni. From them I heard that Susan and Mr. Shaw had been missing ever since Saturday night.

※

Mr. Bodoni had been the last to see them. About ten o'clock Saturday night he had been torn away from his television set by an emergency call from a seventh-floor tenant who was having a lively time with a clogged tub drain and a ruptured hot water faucet. Having averted the flood and calmed the tenant, Mr. Bodoni decided that since his evening's entertainment was ruined anyway he might as well turn the time to account by working his way down floor by floor, checking his mousetraps and collecting newspapers. He reported that he met the Shaws as he was coming along the third-floor hallway.

They were dressed "kinda funny." When pressed for details, he could only state that their clothing struck him as very old-fashioned—"sorta like, well, the Gay Nineties, I guess." Naturally he was a good deal surprised by their appearance; but after staring at them for a while as they waited for the elevator, an answer suggested itself. He grinned around his cigar and said:

"Fancy dress party, hah? Costoom party?"

Mr. Shaw muttered something indistinguishable. He had an air of acute embarrassment. Susan, on the other hand, looked radiant with happiness. She smiled at Mr. Bodoni, who remembered thinking. 'That's a good-looking kid. Wonder where she's been last coupla days? Didn't hurt her none by the looks of it.'

The elevator arrived and the Shaws got in. Susan called out, "Goodbye, Mr. Bodoni!"

"Yeah," he answered. "Have a good time."

It wasn't until a few minutes later that he had second thoughts about his costume party theory. For one thing, the elevator arrow showed that the Shaws had gone straight to the seventh floor. Having just come from the seventh floor himself, he was sure that there was no party going on there. For another thing, Mr. Shaw had been carrying a large black cat, and Susan a book bound in blue leather—neither of them an appropriate object to take to a party . . .

"It don't figure," said Mr. Bodoni, noisily scratching his head. "It just don't figure."

"We'll be lucky if we ever see them again," Mrs. Clutchett sniffled. "You mark my words."

"This checks with Bodoni's story, anyway," Detective Haugen said, showing me a pink slip of paper. It was a receipt from Ace Theatrical Costumers for "1 Victorian gent's outfit." "You know anything about all this?" he asked me.

I started to tell him what I knew, but he cut me short.

"Okay, okay—I already got the girl's story from Mrs. Clutchett here. Hysterical fantasy, that's plain enough. She must have had some kind of traumatic shock. Or else it was a cover-up story for something else. Somebody could have scared her into telling it. Wish I could have questioned her personally, but she kept putting me off." He pulled a small glass vial from his pocket. "Look at that—straw! The girl was shedding straw when she got out of the elevator Saturday morning. Nobody packs things in straw any more."

"She said she was sleeping in a stable," I volunteered promptly.

"I checked on that. The nearest stable is two and a half miles from here, over in the park. Nobody saw her there. The next nearest source of straw is the zoo. Nobody saw her there, either . . . Well, the laboratory boys'll tell us where it came from. Now, do any of you know if Shaw had any enemies?"

Mr. Bodoni, Mrs. Clutchett and I shook our heads. "He looked like the kind of man who wouldn't have an enemy in the world," I said.

"Ahh, you can't go by looks. It's the quiet ones that surprise you. But he's all right with the company he works for—no embezzlement or anything; no apparent worries . . . On the face of it it looks like they were trying to make a getaway. But why would they put on disguises that stick out like sore thumbs, and why they would go *up* the elevator—"

"Yeah," Mr. Bodoni interrupted helpfully. "No party up there, that's for sure."

"—*up* the elevator instead of down, is more than I can figure out. Plus the fact that the girl was missing before . . . I don't know. I can't work out a theory to fit the facts."

"Look," I said, "why don't you proceed on the assumption that they really did go back into the past, just as the girl claimed? That would solve everything."

It was an interesting look they all gave me.

For all I know, Detective Haugen is still trying to work out a theory to fit the facts. You may remember (if you live in this city) that the newspapers had fun with the case for several days. You may even remember that some solemn crank wrote to the editor to state that Susan and her father had been kidnapped by the crew of a flying saucer "for experimental purposes prior to a mass invasion of the major Continents of the Earth." Mrs. Clutchett, finding this hypothesis much more horrendous than anything she could have invented herself, seized upon it as pure gospel. In fact, she has entered into correspondence with the author of it, a retired plumber named Whipsnade; they have given up hope of ever seeing the Shaws again (as I have myself); and nothing that I or anyone else can say will shake their happy conviction that cataclysm from the skies is imminent, and that they are the first to know.

☙

So there the matter stood until a few days ago, when a friend of mine, an officer of the local Historical Association, invited me to have a look at the association's new headquarters.

Someone had left the Association a large sum of money, which had been used to build a meeting room and a suite of offices. The little library-museum was a particularly pleasant room, with its leather-bound books, a genuine Colonial fireplace and mantel, exhibit cases full of pewter, and a Confederate cavalry officer's uniform in an excellent state of preservation. But what drew my special attention was a framed sepia-toned photograph on one wall. It showed a tall narrow house, with towers, and pointed windows, and iron railings around the roof, and gingerbread work everywhere. There was a group of people on the verandah steps, and something about them caught my eye.

"Marvellous old horror, isn't it?" my friend said. "The architecture buffs here practically worship that house. Perfect example of the Hudson River Bracketed style."

"Have any idea where it stood?"

"No, not much. It could have been in your part of town, though, up near Ward Street. One of our oldest members thinks he recalls a house like that out there when he was a boy. Of course it was still open country then."

"Hmm. Is the picture dated?"

"I think so. Eighteen eighty—oh, eighty-three, eighty-four; thereabouts. Here, I can look it up in the catalog."

"Don't bother," I said, "that's close enough. Have you got a magnifying glass around here somewhere?"

"Sure. Just a minute."

He came back with a reading glass, saying, "Have a good look at the scroll-work around the porch. It's priceless."

I am no connoisseur of scroll-work, but I looked at it to please him, and duly pronounced it priceless. But of course it was the people that interested me. The photograph was very grainy; but if I held the glass right and narrowed my eyes, quite a bit of detail could be made out. Here is what I saw:

On the left-hand side of the group stands a boy. He wears a kind of military uniform, and his arms are folded. There is a terrific scowl on his face, which I suppose is intended to quell a whole army of hardened veterans; but a certain well-fed plumpness of feature renders the attempt unsuccessful.

Next to him stands a woman. She is extraordinarily beautiful. There is a bundle in her arms, a great swaddle of blankets and lace concealing what is inside; but from the way she smiles at it there must be a baby—a very warm one, no doubt—under all that covering.

A man stands in the middle of the group. There is something familiar about him, but I cannot and will not swear that it is Mr. Shaw. You must remember that I met him only once, and he had no mustache then. This man does have a mustache, a very imposing one; and behind it is the happy but faintly bewildered expression of one who has been led against his better judgment to the foot of a rainbow, and has found, contrary to all common sense and education, a pot of gold there.

Next to him stands a lovely girl, evidently the woman's daughter. She has the faraway musing look of a confirmed romantic.

With the last figure in the group I am on safe ground. It is Susan, all right. She has not yet graduated to long dresses that go *swish*, but to judge by her figure that happy day is not far off. Looking at her face, I remembered her voice saying to me, when we once went up the elevator together, "I can't make it come out right." But she is no longer puzzling over how many two-hundred-pound people can safely ride in an elevator of 1500 lbs capacity. She has the rather smug little smile of a girl who has undertaken something much more difficult than an arithmetic problem, and has seen it through to her perfect satisfaction.

"I know where that is," I said, giving the glass back to my friend. "You can tell your architecture buffs that that picture was taken on—what did she call it?—Weird Street."

He smiled uncertainly. "What's the joke?"

"Oh, never mind—you wouldn't believe me if I told you."

"Come on," he insisted. "Grinning like a Cheshire cat. What have you got up your sleeve?"

"Patience, patience!" I said. "Maybe I'll write a book about it."

ABOUT THE AUTHOR

Edward Ormondroyd was born in Wilkinsburg, Pennsylvania, and he lived much of his boyhood in Ann Arbor, Michigan. During World War II he spent two years on a destroyer escort in the Pacific. After his war service Mr. Ormondroyd attended the University of California where he received a degree in English. Formerly a Californian, Mr. Ormondroyd now lives in New York State and is a librarian.

ABOUT THE ILLUSTRATOR

Peggie Bach has won numerous awards for her painting and illustration and has exhibited in the San Francisco Museum of Art and the Honolulu Academy of Art. Born in Denmark, she came to this country in 1925. The artist is married and lives with her husband and two sons in Gladwyne, Pennsylvania.

TEENAGERS FACE LIFE AND LOVE

Choose books filled with fun and adventure, discovery and disenchantment, failure and conquest, triumph and tragedy, life and love.

☐	20907	**HIGH AND OUTSIDE** Linnea A. Due	$1.95
☐	20868	**HAUNTED** Judith St. George	$1.75
☐	15096	**DON'T STAND IN THE SOUP**	$1.75
		Jovial Bob Stine	
☐	20646	**THE LATE GREAT ME** Sandra Scoppettone	$2.25
☐	13691	**HOME BEFORE DARK** Sue Ellen Bridgers	$1.75
☐	13671	**ALL TOGETHER NOW** Sue Ellen Bridgers	$1.95
☐	14836	**PARDON ME, YOU'RE STEPPING ON MY EYEBALL!** Paul Zindel	$2.25
☐	20608	**A HOUSE FOR JONNIE O.**	$2.25
		Blossom Elfman	
☐	14306	**ONE FAT SUMMER** Robert Lipsyte	$1.95
☐	14690	**THE CONTENDER** Robert Lipsyte	$2.25
☐	13315	**CHLORIS AND THE WEIRDOS** Linn Platt	$1.95
☐	12577	**GENTLEHANDS** M. E. Kerr	$1.95
☐	20639	**QUEEN OF HEARTS** Bill & Vera Cleaver	$1.95
☐	20759	**MY DARLING, MY HAMBURGER**	$2.25
		Paul Zindel	
☐	20537	**HEY DOLLFACE** Deborah Hautzig	$1.95
☐	20474	**WHERE THE RED FERN GROWS**	$2.50
		Wilson Rawls	
☐	20170	**CONFESSIONS OF A TEENAGE BABOON**	$2.25
		Paul Zindel	
☐	14730	**OUT OF LOVE** Hilma Wolitzer	$1.75
☐	14225	**SOMETHING FOR JOEY** Richard E. Peck	$2.25
☐	14687	**SUMMER OF MY GERMAN SOLDIER**	$2.25
		Bette Greene	
☐	13693	**WINNING** Robin Brancato	$1.95

Buy them at your local bookstore or use this handy coupon for ordering:

Bantam Books, Inc., Dept. EDN, 414 East Golf Road, Des Plaines, Ill. 60016

Please send me the books I have checked above. I am enclosing $_____ (please add $1.00 to cover postage and handling). Send check or money order —no cash or C.O.D.'s please.

Mr/Mrs/Miss _____

Address _____

City _____ State/Zip _____

EDN—4/82

Please allow four to six weeks for delivery. This offer expires 10/82.

DAHL, ZINDEL, AND BRANCATO

Select the best names, the best stories in the world of teenage and young readers books!

Bantam's HI-LO Paperback Series

Hi-Lo Books are designed for teenagers who have been "turned off" by books. Written at a high level of interest, these books deal with contemporary subject matter relating to teenage readers such as music, dating, dancing, school, parents and the supernatural. Dramatic photographs or illustrations on every other page keep up reader involvement.

☐ 20382	THE HEADLESS ROOMMATE AND OTHER TALES OF TERROR D. Cohen	$1.85
☐ 14824	BERMUDA TRIANGLE/ MYSTERIES OF NATURE E. Dolan	$1.50
☐ 14620	CUTTING A RECORD IN NASHVILLE L. Van Ryzin	$1.50
☐ 14618	DISCO KID C. Gathje	$1.50
☐ 14619	THE HITCHHIKERS P. Thompson	$1.50
☐ 14938	INCREDIBLE CRIMES L. Atkinson	$1.50
☐ 14822	ONE DARK NIGHT W. White	$1.50
☐ 14832	PSYCHIC STORIES STRANGE, BUT TRUE L. Atkinson	$1.50
☐ 14621	ROCK FEVER E. Rabinowich	$1.50